A HIGHLAND BETROTHAL

Highland Bodyguards, Book 4.5

EMMA PRINCE

Books by Emma Prince

Highland Bodyguards Series:

The Lady's Protector (Book 1)

Heart's Thief (Book 2)

A Warrior's Pledge (Book 3)

Claimed by the Bounty Hunter (Book 4)

A Highland Betrothal (Novella, Book 4.5)

The Promise of a Highlander (Book 5)

The Bastard Laird's Bride (Book 6—Reid Mackenzie's story) coming Fall 2017!

The Sinclair Brothers Trilogy:

Highlander's Ransom (Book 1)

Highlander's Redemption (Book 2)

Highlander's Return (Bonus Novella, Book 2.5)

Highlander's Reckoning (Book 3)

Viking Lore Series:

Enthralled (Viking Lore, Book 1)

Shieldmaiden's Revenge (Viking Lore, Book 2)

The Bride Prize (Viking Lore, Book 2.5)

Desire's Hostage (Viking Lore, Book 3)

Thor's Wolf (Viking Lore, Book 3.5)—a Kindle Worlds novella

Other Books:

Wish upon a Winter Solstice (A Highland Holiday Novella)

A Highland Betrothal

HIGHLAND BODYGUARDS, BOOK 4.5

~

By
Emma Prince

A Highland Betrothal (Highland Bodyguards, Book 4.5)
Copyright © 2017 by Emma Prince

All rights reserved. No part of this publication may be reproduced, distributed, or transmitted in any form or by any means, or stored in a database or retrieval system, without the prior written permission of the author except in the case of brief quotations embodied in critical articles and reviews. For more information, contact emmaprincebooks@gmail.com.

This is a work of fiction. Names, characters, organizations, places, events, and incidents are the products of the author's imagination or are used fictitiously. Any resemblance to actual events or persons, living or dead, is entirely coincidental.
Updated 7/10/17

For Scott. Always.

Chapter One

July, 1318
Lochmaben, Scottish Lowlands

A soft rap sounded against the wooden pole holding up the far end of the canvas tent.

"Enter." Graeme MacKay didn't bother lifting his head from the cot to see who was here to pester him. Only one man came to visit him anymore.

"It's the middle of the day, man. What are ye still doing in bed?"

Though Colin MacKay, Graeme's cousin, had merely repeated the same query he used nigh every day, Graeme still muttered a curse.

"Ye ken why."

"Nay, I ken that the sun is shining. I ken that the air is sweet and warm. I ken that the others are on the practice field, where they have been training since dawn—where *ye* should have been since dawn. This is the camp for Robert the Bruce's army, after all, no' some summer retreat for the infirm."

Graeme finally propped his forearm under his head and looked at his cousin. Though Colin's words had been cutting, he wore an easy smile, and his bright blue gaze cajoled Graeme with the MacKay charm.

The MacKay charm that Graeme distinctly lacked.

"What the bloody hell do ye want?" he snapped. "For me to stand up without struggling, walk without a damned cane, and magically be able to practice with the others again?"

Graeme sat up a little more to absently rub the blasted right thigh that had left him in this state. Suddenly Graeme noticed that Colin held something behind his back. He narrowed his eyes at his cousin, but Colin didn't seem to notice.

"I dinnae expect the impossible," Colin said levelly. "But I do expect ye to quit yer wallowing and act like the warrior ye are."

Graeme ground his teeth together. "I'm no' wallowing." As soon as the words were out, he cursed himself. He sounded like a petulant bairn even to his own ears.

Colin lifted a golden brow at him, that damned charming smile coming to his mouth once more. "Oh, aye? Then prove me wrong."

Colin moved one hand out from behind his back to reveal a sword. Before Graeme realized what his cousin was about, the blade came sailing across the tent toward him.

Graeme twisted his body out of the way even as his hand shot out from beneath his head and snagged the flying sword by the hilt.

"What the bloody he—"

Colin whipped a second sword from behind his back. Without warning, he charged at Graeme where he lay on the cot, sword raised for a deadly strike.

With no time to stand or even breathe a curse at his mad cousin, Graeme flung his blade up to block Colin's attack. The sound of metal on metal rang sharply through the little tent. These were no wooden practice swords or blunted blades meant for friendly training. Nay, they were very real—and very sharp.

Graeme rolled off the cot, landing with a whoosh of breath on the hard-packed dirt floor. He kept rolling until he'd crossed to Colin's left side. Then using his good leg, he kicked at Colin's knees, knocking him off-balance.

Colin staggered back, fighting to keep his footing. Graeme used the moment of reprieve to get his good leg under him and hoist himself to standing. He winced as his weight came down on his right leg, but he refused to lower the tip of his sword to the ground and lean on it like a cane.

Knowing he needed to save his energy for a single defeating blow, Graeme waited for Colin to advance again. Colin regained his balance at last, then moved in slowly, that cursed smile quirking his lips.

Colin feigned left, then went straight for Graeme's bad leg. In the back of his mind, Graeme tucked away a reminder to punch his cousin squarely in the smiling face later. But now, he didn't have time for that.

Graeme barely managed to block the blow. He took a hobbling step backward, letting his blade slide against Colin's. With a sudden flick of the wrist, he locked their swords together and pinned Colin's to the ground. Grinding his teeth against the ache, Graeme bolted forward, driving his shoulder into Colin's midsection.

Colin tumbled backward, the momentum forcing him to release his grip on his pinned sword. He landed with a grunt on his back. Before he could rise, Graeme positioned the point of his blade at Colin's throat.

Blue eyes dancing with merriment, Colin held up his hands in surrender. Just as Graeme lowered the sword, Colin's mouth split into his widest grin yet.

"I hate to break it to ye, cousin," he said,

dusting himself off as he rose to his feet, "but ye just proved me right. The fact that ye were able to best me shows that ye *have* been wallowing these past few weeks."

Now was the perfect opportunity to drive his fist into his cousin's grinning mouth, but suddenly Graeme could no longer muster his anger. He hobbled to the cot and sank down with a muffled groan, propping the sword next to him.

"I didnae mean to be harsh," Colin said. "I only meant to prove to ye that ye neednae remain in this dark, cramped tent all day. Ye are still a warrior, yer injury be damned."

Colin drew the lone wooden chair in Graeme's tent toward the cot and sat down. When Graeme looked up, he found that for the first time since entering, Colin no longer smiled.

"Still no word from Anna?"

Graeme exhaled sharply. He would much rather face a surprise attack from Colin MacKay, one of Robert the Bruce's most skilled and trusted warriors, than speak of Anna Ross.

"Nay, and I dinnae expect to hear from her again."

"Then ye ken about the reading of the banns?"

Graeme's fists clenched at his sides. Aye, he'd heard the announcement of Anna Ross's engagement—to Laird Donald Munro. "Tomorrow marks the third Sunday."

The third and *final* Sunday that Anna's impending union with the Munro Laird would be announced, and the last chance for someone to come forward and declare any objection to the marriage.

Though it made Graeme's chest contract to admit it, there was no sound reason for him to proclaim that Anna could not wed Laird Munro. Aye, he'd already asked Anna to marry him. But she had never answered.

Colin cleared his throat, shifting slightly in his chair. "I ken it isnae my place to ask, but…what happened? Damn near every soul in the Highlands kens that ye were courting Anna Ross."

Graeme shoved down the anger and hurt that rose thickly in his throat. Anna was marrying another. He needed to harden himself against any lingering emotion he had for her.

"There isnae much to tell, really," he replied, straining to sound casual. "I wrote to her no' long after the siege at Berwick. I told her that I'd made it out of the woods with the fever, but that the injury to my leg might never fully heal. Despite the fact that my scar is unsightly and I'll likely have a limp for the rest of my life, I asked her to marry me."

Graeme exhaled slowly. Aye, he'd told her about being injured at Berwick, then the terrible, life-sapping fever that had set in, followed by an infection that might have claimed his leg—or his life—if the camp's healer, Jossalyn Sinclair, hadn't cut away a crabapple-sized chunk of flesh from his thigh.

But he'd told her much more than that, too. He'd shown her his heart—all of it. When he'd been lying on the verge of death, fighting against the raging fever and the putrescence that had spread from the arrow wound, all he'd thought of was Anna.

Her golden hair brighter than the sun.

Her deep blue eyes like the sky on a perfect Highland summer day.

Her rosy lips, which curved in a smile whenever he was about to kiss her.

He'd told her that she was his life, his heart. He'd said that when he'd thought he was on death's threshold, he'd prayed only to be able to see her once more. And he'd asked that if he somehow managed to survive, that she make him the luckiest man in all the world and marry him.

Such words did not come easily to a man like Graeme. He was known for his skills with a blade, not bare-spoken declarations of love.

"And…and she refused ye?" Colin asked softly.

Graeme felt his mouth tighten. Of course he'd known that when he confessed that he was a changed man, she might hesitate to agree to wed him. When he'd wooed her, he'd been a proud and strong warrior. Now when he bothered to rise from his cot, he leaned heavily on a cane. Gone was the fierce Highlander he'd been before the siege on Berwick back in April, and in his place was a broken man.

Still, he had at least expected to get an answer to his missive. A plea to delay any questions of marriage, mayhap, or a gentle rejection at worst.

Instead, he'd been met with naught but silence.

"Nay," he said flatly. "She never replied."

"And ye are sure yer missive reached the lass?"

"The King himself sent one of his messengers with my note," Graeme replied tightly. "The Bruce said it was the least he could do for the man who'd nearly given his leg in the service of reclaiming Berwick from the English. The missive was delivered directly into Anna's hand, according to the messenger."

Graeme rolled his shoulders, a move that was half meant to relieve the tension there and half meant to appear like a disaffected shrug. "I can only assume that once she heard about my injury, she no longer wanted aught to do with me. A man who can barely walk doesnae make a good warrior—or a good husband."

Colin made a little noise with his tongue, his brows dropping. "I find it hard to believe that Anna would be so fickle. She always seemed like a steady lass to me. Isnae it more likely that old bear of a father she has wasnae keen on his only daughter dallying with a MacKay? If that were the case, the lass's engagement to Laird Munro makes even more sense."

Graeme had considered that when the shock at hearing the news of Anna's engagement had cleared a bit. Laird William Ross, Anna's father, had never been overly pleased with Anna and Graeme's courtship.

Graeme wasn't the son of a Laird, but that was the least of his problems. The MacKays and Rosses, though near-neighbors, had been on tense terms for years. The MacKays were allied with the Sutherlands, who bordered the Rosses. The Sutherlands and Rosses had frequent disputes over lands and sheep, and the way the Ross Laird saw things, the MacKays, as friends of his enemies the Sutherlands, were his adversaries as well.

"The fact is," Graeme said, "it doesnae matter. Mayhap Anna didnae want me. Mayhap her father wished to strengthen his alliance with the Munros. Whatever the case, Anna is naught to me now."

As an uncomfortable silence fell in the tent, Graeme sensed Colin's sharp gaze on him. He crossed his arms over his chest defensively, but when he looked up, he found Colin in a rare moment of uncertainty.

"What?" Graeme demanded bluntly. Aye, somehow he'd been passed over when the MacKay charm had been doled out. Colin could befriend a man with a single smile or a companionable pound on the shoulder. Graeme, on the other hand, was more likely to offend than charm with his brusqueness and lack of finesse.

The hesitancy fled from Colin's face as he seemed to decide something. "I didnae just come here for a social call."

"Aye, ye came to draw a sword on an injured man," Graeme shot back.

Colin snorted, his playful half-smile returning. "Well, aye. But there was a reason for that." He grew sober, and Graeme felt himself stiffen with unease.

"Ye see, I have an assignment for ye, and I had to be sure ye could complete it," Colin said.

Graeme felt his brows drop, but before he could interrupt, Colin hurried on.

"Ye ken that I work for the Bruce in his Bodyguard Corps."

Word had begun to spread through Robert the Bruce's army about an elite group of warriors. They were said to work on special orders from the King himself to protect those most vulnerable to the underhanded tactics of the English, who had been targeting individuals important to the Scottish cause for independence since the Battle of Bannockburn four years past.

Graeme nodded slowly. "Aye. It is a great honor for ye—for all MacKays, really—that the King has placed so much trust in ye, Colin."

"The Bruce is always looking for good men to join the Corps." Colin fixed Graeme with a pointed look, his brows raised in a silent query.

Graeme's jaw slackened as realization dawned. "Is this some sort of sick joke, cousin?" He waved a hand at his right thigh. The wound was covered by his breeches, but they both knew very well what had happened to him—and the permanent damage that had likely been done.

Jossalyn had done all she could. Aye, she'd saved Graeme's leg—and his life, most likely—but the divot in his thigh where the flesh had to be cut away was knotted over in an unsightly scar, and he would likely limp for the rest of his days.

Colin held up a hand. "We need good fighters, aye, but we also need men with wits, courage, and honor as well. Ye more than proved yerself to possess all those things and more at Berwick. And even with yer leg the way it is, ye just verified what I've suspected for more than a month now."

"Oh, aye?" Graeme bit out. "And what is that?"

"That ye are more capable than ye are letting on—mayhap even more than ye believe yerself to be."

"What, because I knocked ye on yer arse? That doesnae mean—"

"I ken why ye've been keeping to yer tent," Colin cut in. "Yer recovery has been slow and difficult, aye, but ye didnae truly quit trying until the announcement of the banns for Anna and Laird Munro."

Graeme glared hard at his cousin, but Colin went on, unperturbed. "I believe that if ye got up and about, worked with the sword a bit, ye'd gain more movement and strength in that leg. And even if ye never get an ounce better, ye just demonstrated that ye can still knock me on my arse, as ye said."

Though he remained silent, Graeme let his hand fall to his leg once more to massage the muscle just above the large scar. He wouldn't admit it to Colin, but he'd suspected the same thing about his recovery.

He'd been making slow but steady progress in regaining his strength and range of motion before he'd heard the news of Anna's engagement. In the weeks that had followed, he'd sunken into a sullen ill temper, refusing to leave his tent or even his cot. The leg had grown worse in that time, making his limp more pronounced and the dull ache more constant.

"I've said as much to the Bruce," Colin added. "And I've also told him that I think ye should join the Bodyguard Corps."

Graeme's hand stilled in its motion on his thigh. This wasn't some cruel trick, then. Colin was serious.

"Ye said ye had a mission in mind for me," Graeme said carefully. "What is it?"

When Colin faltered for the second time in as many moments, Graeme knew he would not like what he was about to hear.

"Ye ken that after the banns are read for the third time tomorrow, Anna will wed Laird Munro," Colin began tentatively.

"Aye," Graeme nearly snarled.

"Well, Munro is no' on his lands. In fact, he is on his way to Lochmaben as we speak."

"The bastard is coming *here*?" Without thinking, Graeme jerked to his feet, only to wince at the throbbing in his leg. With a huff, he lowered himself to the edge of the cot once more but did not take his gaze from Colin.

"Just because he is marrying Anna doesnae make him a bastard," Colin said dryly. "But aye, he's coming here. The Bruce called him and a few other Lairds down to discuss the state of things in the Highlands. What with establishing Berwick as a Scottish stronghold once more and continuing our advance along the Borderlands, the King hasnae had time to speak to the Lairds or visit the Highlands in quite some time. As ye can imagine, even those clans united behind the Bruce still lose sight of our larger goals and revert back to in-fighting now and again."

Graeme nodded curtly. Despite being on the same side of the war against the English, many Highland clans still wasted their energies on petty clan feuds. The MacKays and the Rosses were a perfect example of that.

"What does Munro's arrival in Lochmaben have to do with me?" he asked. Suddenly a horrifying thought occurred to him. "Dinnae tell me ye want me to guard the man set to marry Anna."

"Nay," Colin said quickly, but when he hesitated, Graeme sensed that his mission would actually be far worse than that.

"Munro doesnae want to wait overlong to wed Anna," Colin went on. "Both clans are counting on the alliance, and Munro wants no uncertainty that they are united. He has requested that Anna join him in the Lowlands once the banns are read for the final time tomorrow so that they can be wed while Munro is here meeting with the Bruce."

A sickening knot formed in the pit of Graeme's stomach. He knew what was coming, but he did not stop Colin from speaking the terrible words.

"Munro wishes to ensure every precaution is taken to see Anna safely to the Lowlands," Colin said. "Times being uncertain and unstable as they are, in addition to an escort of Ross and Munro soldiers, Munro requested that the Bruce provide one of his best warriors to see to Anna's protection."

There it was. Graeme was supposed to deliver Anna, the only woman he'd ever loved, to the arms of another man. Graeme looked down to find that his hands were clenched so tight that his knuckles had turned white.

"I recommended ye for the assignment," Colin finished quietly.

"Why?" Graeme growled, his gaze pinning Colin.

Instead of retreating from the daggers Graeme was shooting at him with his eyes, Colin met his stare directly. "Because I need ye back."

Graeme blinked, breaking his glare. "What?"

"I need ye back—the version of ye that is a warrior, a Highlander, a MacKay." Colin leaned forward in the chair, propping his elbows on his knees. "Ye can still walk, which means ye can still ride, too. Ye can still wield a sword. Yet here ye hide." He swept a hand around to indicate the little tent. "It isnae yer leg that's stopping ye—it is yer heart."

Graeme's jaw worked for a moment as he struggled for words. "So what if it is?" he managed weakly at last. "So what if I dinnae want to see Anna ever again, let alone escort her to her fiancé?"

From the look of sympathy that flashed in Colin's blue eyes, he knew he had Graeme on his heels now—and Graeme knew it too. Colin was right—he'd been wallowing, and not because of his injury, but because of a broken heart. If he kept hiding in his tent and sullenly refusing to return to training, soon he would not only have a broken heart, but a broken spirit as well.

"Ye ken what I went through with Joan," Colin said softly.

The whole clan knew. Colin had once been handfasted to Joan, the most beguiling and sought-after lass in the Highlands. But while Colin had been away fighting for the Bruce, Joan had taken up with Colin's best friend. Colin had caught them rolling in the hay together. After that, the normally easy-going and even-keeled Colin turned untrusting and suspicious, though he usually managed to cover it up with a smile or a joke.

"Sometimes the best way to move on from someone also happens to be the most painful way," Colin said. "But mayhap seeing Anna and accepting her as Laird Munro's fiancée will help ye heal and get on with things."

That was easy for Colin to say given the fact that Joan's betrayal had eventually led him to a far better match—and a far better life. Colin had been lucky enough to fall in love again. Sabine MacKay, his wife, had healed Colin's heart and brought back the lighter-hearted man he'd once been.

Yet Graeme held no expectation of being as fortunate as Colin. He'd already found the love of his life. And now she was marrying someone else.

But Colin was right about one thing—Graeme had to accept that Anna was no longer his. He was tired of hiding, tired of floundering in his own self-pity. Aye, mayhap he needed to face this—face *her*—one last time before he could put her in his past for good.

"When do I leave?" he asked flatly.

Colin's sandy blond brows rose slightly. It seemed from his expression that he had managed to surprise himself with his MacKay powers of persuasion. "Once the banns are read for the final time tomorrow, Laird Ross will send her southward. Munro's guards will have likely already been sent to Ross lands to ensure her journey goes smoothly."

"I'd better leave today, then," Graeme said, rising. "If I ride hard, I'll intercept them only a day or two into their trek. Besides," he said, picking up the sword Colin had thrown at him. "If I leave now, I willnae have to lay eyes on Laird Munro."

Colin snorted as he, too, rose to his feet. "That would likely be for the best. We have enough to worry about without ye starting a new feud between the MacKays and the Munros."

His face growing serious, Colin clapped a hand on Graeme's shoulder.

"It is good to have ye back to yer old self, cousin."

Aye, Graeme thought as he quickly readied himself for his journey into the Highlands. It was good to be back.

Chapter Two

"Safe travels, my dearest."

Anna and her father crossed under the open portcullis and came to a halt just outside the Ross clan castle's stone curtain wall.

Anna blinked back the tears that were making her father wobble before her eyes, but she could not seem to dislodge the lump filling her throat.

Laird William Ross's gray brows drew together and his lips compressed behind his beard. She must be failing utterly at putting on a brave face, for her father's concern was clearly written across his features.

"It...it will be fine, I'm sure, Father," she managed at last.

Aye, the journey was unlikely to be eventful—not with the dozen guards, a mixture of Ross men and Munros, who'd be escorting her to the

Lowlands. Still, Anna could not seem to find her faith in the words she'd just used to reassure her father. Even if she arrived in Lochmaben to wed Laird Munro without incident, she would not be fine. Not at all.

A knot of tangled emotion once again tightened her throat. How could she ever be fine again when she knew that Graeme MacKay wished to marry her, yet she was marrying another?

Anna's features had always been easy to read, and despite her efforts to rein in her emotions, now was apparently no exception. Her father took her hands in his much larger, grizzled ones and squeezed hard, his eyes sad as he held her tear-filled gaze.

"Ye ken I dinnae want to see ye hurt, dearest," he murmured. "Yer tears are daggers to my heart. But I must do what is right for the future—for the clan."

They'd been through this before. Countless times. Anna knew her father loved her and valued her happiness, but he simply could not set aside the clan's welfare when it came to making the decision of whom she would wed.

As the only daughter of a Highland Laird, Anna had been raised to accept the fact that her husband would be chosen for her, and that strategic alliances, not love, would dictate that decision.

She had never planned, therefore, to fall in love

with Graeme, a warrior rather than a Laird, and a MacKay rather than a Munro or a Mackenzie or someone from one of the other more powerful neighboring clans.

Yet fallen in love she had. She'd lived the last two years as if she were caught in a perpetual spring. The sun seemed brighter and warmer when Graeme was near. The flowers smelled sweeter. The grasses felt softer underfoot.

But as always in the Highlands, even the most promising, glorious spring could be ruined by the swift, brutal strike of a late-breaking storm.

That storm had broken two months past. On the same day she'd received the missive in which Graeme had spread his heart at her feet and asked her to marry him, her father had knocked softly on her chamber door and informed her that he would begin seeking an engagement between her and Laird Donald Munro.

Munro was a kind enough man from what she remembered of his visit to Ross lands several years past. Yet he was twice Anna's age, and he bore a serious, formal air that had made her feel ill at ease around him.

Anna had wept herself to sleep that night. Her father had wrung his hands and paced with worry, for he'd been taken aback by how strongly Anna reacted. He'd tried to reassure her that everything would be fine, but with each of his attempts, she only wept harder—for herself, but also for Graeme.

His letter had broken her heart with his words about how greatly he'd struggled and how close he'd come to death. But then it had mended it back together again when he'd written that he loved her more than ever before and wished to join their lives forever.

When her tears had dried enough that they no longer made the ink run, she wrote him a reply. But her father had gently told her that he would not allow the missive to be sent. It was best to let a broken heart heal swiftly, he'd told her. Once he could make the arrangements, she would marry Laird Munro. There was no good to be had from drawing out her pain, or the MacKay lad's, he'd insisted.

In the long, monotonous days and lonely, tear-filled nights since then, however, the wound in her heart hadn't healed. If anything, it gaped larger and rawer.

She knew standing before her father now that he saw it too. His kind, worried blue eyes betrayed the knowledge that Anna might not ever heal properly from this pain.

But that didn't change her duty—to her father, to her clan, and to Laird Munro.

Anna dragged in a ragged breath and pulled her spine up. If she left like this, a mess of tears and quivering lips, her father would never forgive himself for doing only what was required of him as Laird.

Their people needed this union. The Rosses and Munros had always been on good terms, but the Highlands remained a volatile and unstable region politically. Shoring up alliances to protect against future uncertainties was always wise.

"I ken ye are doing yer duty to the clan," she said, willing her voice to be steady and strong. "And now I must do my duty as well."

"I only wish that I could see ye smile on yer wedding day," her father said, his eyes shining with unshed tears.

Before she completely lost her composure, Anna threw her arms around her father and hugged him fiercely.

"I promise to smile," she murmured against his shoulder. "A *real* smile."

When Anna stepped back, her father cleared his throat of its thickness and blinked back the tears from his eyes.

"Ye will have the finest escort. I saw to that," he said, motioning her toward the large group of men clustered a stone's throw beyond the castle wall.

Most of the men sat on horseback, waiting for her to finish her goodbyes. All of them wore variations of red plaid around their hips and across their shoulders. The Munros' burgundy wool with thin yellow and green stripes was interspersed with the familiar green-checked crimson plaids of the Rosses.

It was reassuring to be among so many braw warriors, yet her mind leapt to an image of the MacKay colors Graeme wore when he was in the Highlands. The dark blues and greens of his clan colors would stand out in this sea of red. Mayhap that was fate telling her it was never meant to be, that they didn't belong together, but some small, defiant part of her rejected such a thought.

"Jerome Munro here will make sure yer journey goes smoothly." Her father motioned one of the men forward. A tall, dark-haired man dismounted and approached.

"Jerome is Laird Munro's most trusted warrior," her father said. "The Laird assures me that ye'll be in good hands with him looking after ye."

"My lady," Jerome said tersely, giving her a curt bow.

Anna couldn't help shrinking back slightly under the hard warrior's brusque manner.

"We'd best be going," Jerome said, glancing at Anna's father. "We are losing daylight, and Laird Munro expects his bride to be delivered in a sennight. Traveling with *that* will slow us down."

Jerome stepped aside and jutted his thumb toward a mule-drawn carriage that Anna hadn't noticed behind the horses and men.

She inhaled. "Father, did ye do this?" She whipped around to find her father smiling down at her.

"Aye. Consider it a wedding present. I hoped to make ye as comfortable as possible for the journey."

Despite her best efforts to control herself, tears once more flooded her eyes and she hugged her father tight again.

Ever since she'd lost control of a horse as a ten-year-old lass, she'd been uncomfortable around horses—in truth, she was plain afraid of them. She'd been dreading having to ride for seven long days on the journey from the Ross keep to the Lowlands where Laird Munro would be waiting. Now at least one small part of her fears for this trip had been allayed.

With one final hug for her father, she forced herself to let him go. She followed Jerome toward the carriage. It was more of a wagon, really, with a man sitting on a bench at the front to guide the harnessed mules. The bottom portion of the wagon was wood, with stretched canvas covering the top. Canvas flaps on the sides meant she could look outside on the journey or keep them closed against inclement weather. It was the finest way she could ever imagine traveling.

She watched as her one small trunk of clothes was loaded into the wagon. Then once Jerome helped her up and into the back, she crawled across the padded bottom to one of the canvas flaps. She pulled it back and waved to her father as Jerome whistled and the men got underway.

"All will be well, dearest," her father called as the wagon creaked and rocked into motion, then began bumping down the path away from the castle.

When at last her father had drawn out of sight, she let the flap fall and brought trembling fingers to her heart. Through the dark blue wool of her simple traveling dress, she felt the crinkle of parchment. Feeling her heart beat against the two missives tucked into her dress, she prayed that her father was right.

Chapter Three

The next day, Anna clenched the wooden sides of the wagon in a white-knuckled grip.

Mayhap she'd made a terrible error in assuming that riding in a wagon would be preferable to traveling on horseback. Aye, the thought of approaching one of the enormous steeds her guards rode still sent shivers of fear through her, but at least if she were on horseback, her bones wouldn't be aching, her head wouldn't be throbbing, and her teeth wouldn't feel as though they were being rattled right out of her skull.

But what else had she expected when traveling by wagon over the rough, uneven roads of the Highlands?

She hadn't gotten any reprieve from the wagon last night, either, for Jerome had insisted that she sleep inside it for her own safety and comfort. Anna had weakly commented that she wouldn't mind sleeping under the stars with her guards, but Jerome had given her a hard look and said that as Laird Munro's bride, she was not to sleep among the men or on the ground.

Though she'd slept well enough, the hours of lying in the motionless wagon hadn't been enough to undo the effects of the jarring ride from the day before. She woke sore and aching, only to hurriedly break her fast before Jerome urged them onward just after dawn.

Now as dusk approached, Anna said a prayer of thanks that they would halt soon—and that two of the seven days of travel were over.

Anna pulled back one of the canvas flaps and peered out into the darkening forest surrounding them. The evening air was filled with the clop of horses' hooves on the packed dirt road, the jangle of harnesses, and the groan of leather as the men shifted in their saddles.

A soft breeze blew mild, fresh air into the wagon. Anna dragged in a lungful, savoring the sweet smells of the summer evening.

Just then a rustling shook the underbrush off to the right of the convoy. It was different than the gentle sway of the trees in the breeze. Nay, this was more concentrated. Louder. And close.

Jerome and the others whipped their heads toward the rustling. The air suddenly felt thick with tension. The wagon came to an abrupt halt, and the sound of steel swords hissing from their sheaths rang in Anna's ears.

"Get down," Jerome snapped at her over his shoulder as he reined his horse in front of the wagon. "And close that bloody flap."

Anna immediately dropped the canvas flap and flattened herself against the padded floor of the wagon. Her breaths came short, her pulse pounding in her ears as she strained to hear what was happening beyond the wagon's cover.

"Show yerself!" Jerome's hard voice boomed out, making Anna jump.

She heard the rustling again, and then a low male voice responded.

"Stand down," the man said. "I am no' yer enemy."

A tingling awareness that was both cold and hot raced up Anna's spine. Was that…?

"Who are ye?" Jerome barked. "And answer quickly."

"I was sent by Robert the Bruce and yer Laird Munro," the man said.

He was closer now. There was no more room to be mistaken. But it couldn't be. Anna's heart leapt into her throat. Could it? She would never forget that voice, the low, gruff Highland lilt she knew so well.

"What is yer business here?" Jerome demanded,

but he no longer shouted, which meant that the man who'd approached was right next to him—right next to the wagon.

She heard the creak of leather as someone dismounted.

"The King and yer Laird requested that I join the retinue," the man said. Aye, it was him. Anna knew it, yet her brain could not seem to make sense of that fact. She kept trying to come up with an explanation for what he was doing here, but her thoughts scattered like leaves in the wind.

"To protect *her*." Suddenly the canvas at the back of the wagon was yanked back, and none other than Graeme MacKay stared at her through the blue light of dusk.

She opened her mouth to speak, but no words came. Like a fool, she stared, slack-jawed and wide-eyed, at Graeme.

He lifted one sandy blond eyebrow at her, though his eyes were as hard and cold as chips of emerald.

"Surprised to see me again, lass?"

Chapter Four

Graeme stared at Anna, trying to keep his teeth clamped together. If he didn't, he feared his jaw would hang as loose as hers did at present.

She was just as beautiful as he remembered—nay, more so. Though the inside of the covered wagon was dimmer than the dusky evening outside, her golden hair still shone lustrously. Her dark blue eyes were wide with surprise, her pink lips parted.

Her hand fluttered to her heart in what appeared to be an unconscious gesture of shock. His gaze dropped down to the lush curve of her breast just below her hand, and unwanted heat suddenly surged through him.

Biting down on a curse, he ripped his gaze away from Anna.

"Why would Laird Munro send ye?" the man

who seemed to be in charge of the convoy said, his dark eyes narrowing on Graeme. "Or the King, for that matter?"

"And ye are?" Graeme returned, grateful to have someone else to focus on besides Anna.

The man's already rigid body went straighter. "Jerome Munro, the Laird's second in command."

"Graeme MacKay." Graeme didn't bother extending his forearm. Instead, he gave Jerome a curt nod. "As to why I'm here, as I said, I'm just following orders. I was sent to protect the lass on her journey. Yer Laird seemed to think that ye and the others weren't enough."

Jerome's nostrils flared, his eyes blazing at the insult. Graeme wouldn't apologize, though. Aye, he was blunt, but that didn't make him wrong.

"I am to join the King's Bodyguard Corps," Graeme went on. "He thought this would be a good first assignment, seeing as how the lass needs to reach the Lowlands safely for yer clans' alliance to go forward."

Jerome huffed a little exhale. "Aye, well." He slowly re-sheathed his sword, and the other guards followed. "Ye may have been sent by the King, but I am in charge of this mission."

Dropping his voice, Jerome stepped closer. "Dinnae question me or get in the way, else even the King's favor willnae protect ye from my wrath."

Graeme considered stepping nose to nose with

Jerome and testing just how far the surly Munro commander could be pushed, but instead he gave another brusque nod.

"We might as well make camp for the night," Jerome said, raising his voice so that the others could hear him once more. He turned to his horse and began unsaddling the animal, and the men did the same, though some sent sideways glances at Graeme.

"Graeme."

He whipped his head around at the soft, velvety voice that still haunted his dreams.

Anna had apparently recovered somewhat from her shock at seeing him, for her bonny mouth no longer hung open. Her rounded gaze was still fixed on him as she scooted forward across the wagon's bottom, however.

When she reached the edge of the wagon, she brought trembling fingers up to her lips. "Is it true? Were ye sent here to escort me to the Lowlands?"

Graeme's hand clenched around the canvas he still held back from the wagon's opening. "Aye."

He saw her mouth curve into a wobbling smile behind her fingertips.

"I ken ye cannae be genuinely happy to see me, so ye must be smiling in discomfort," he said, his voice hard and low.

It was a trait he used to find charming and endearing. Whenever Anna felt uncomfortable or awkward, a nervous smile would take control of her delicate features.

When he'd discovered this little quirk, he'd quickly developed a love of teasing her about it, trying to find ways to make that lopsided grin appear on her lips. He'd once lifted his kilt and flashed his naked arse at her just to win one of those silly smiles. Another time he'd broken into song in the middle of a busy market square, bellowing off-key at the top of his lungs as she shushed him and covered her smile with one hand.

Now, as she fought against the strained curve of her lips, his heart twisted painfully. Aye, it was nerves and not happiness that made her smile. No doubt she'd hoped never to encounter him again. How awkward this must be for her, to have her former beau escorting her to her new fiancé.

"I-I never thought I'd see ye again," she murmured.

"Aye," Graeme ground out, hardening himself against the soft caress of her voice. "Yer silence after my last missive made yer wishes clear."

Her hand dropped from her mouth and once again fluttered to the spot just above her heart. "Graeme, we need to talk. I need to tell ye—"

"MacKay." Jerome's sharp voice cut Anna off. The Munro commander strode to the back of the wagon where Graeme lingered.

"Lady Anna, ye need yer rest," Jerome said

evenly, keeping his dark gaze fixed on Graeme. "We have another long day of travel ahead of us, and the wagon can only go so fast."

Jerome's eyes flicked briefly to Anna. "See to yer needs for the night, my lady," he said curtly. "Then return to the wagon and sleep while ye can." His gaze slid back to Graeme. "I need to apprise MacKay here of our route."

Jerome jerked his head to the side, indicating that Graeme step away with him. Reluctantly, Graeme released his hold on the wagon's canvas covering and moved off.

He gritted his teeth against the ache in his leg from riding. Though he tried to smooth out his gait, he felt both Jerome and Anna's eyes on him as he limped several paces away.

Once they were off to the side, Jerome waited for Anna to slip unassisted from the wagon and receive a portion of biscuits and dried meat from one of the other men. Against his will, Graeme's gaze followed Anna as she moved through the little camp the guards were making.

"Graeme MacKay," Jerome said, quiet enough that no one else could overhear. "I've heard of ye before. Ye were the man courting Lady Anna before her engagement to Laird Munro."

Though Jerome's tone was soft, Graeme didn't miss the subtle edge to it—or the unspoken warning. He turned fully to Jerome, meeting his gaze evenly.

"Aye, I was."

"And now Lady Anna will wed my Laird," Jerome went on, his voice hardening. "So there is no place for ye here. Mayhap ye should have stayed away."

"I'm just following orders," Graeme ground out. "It was yer Laird who requested that the King send a member of his Bodyguard Corps."

Out of the corner of his eye, Graeme noticed Anna moving toward the wagon once more. She wearily hoisted herself back into it and scooted through the canvas flaps. When the flaps closed, she was cut off from his gaze, but his eyes lingered on the gently swaying canvas for a moment.

He turned back to find Jerome watching him as a hawk eyed its prey.

"Ye are devoted to yer clan—yer Laird—are ye no', MacKay?"

The question was spoken lightly—deceptively so.

"Aye."

"So am I," Jerome said. "I'd give my life for my people—or *take* life. My Laird wants Lady Anna to be delivered safely to him. He wishes to marry her. So as his most loyal warrior, I'll see both done."

Jerome shifted just a hair closer, but the air suddenly felt thick with the unspoken promise of aggression. "And I willnae let *anyone* get in the way of doing my duty. Ye understand, MacKay?"

"I have no intention of interfering," Graeme replied tightly. "We are on the same side for once, Munro."

A long moment passed, and Graeme felt his whole body pulling tauter than a bow string.

At last, Jerome rocked back slightly on his heels. "Good," he said. "I'm glad we understand each other."

Jerome stalked off toward the others as they began to bed down on the ground, wrapping themselves in their Munro and Ross plaids.

Graeme walked slowly back to where he'd left his horse, trying to work the knots out of both his leg and his head.

He removed the saddle and bridle from his horse and tethered the animal among the others on the edge of their little camp, but even after he'd drawn an extra length of plaid from his saddlebags and settled on the ground with the other men, his mind was still a tangled mess.

He thought he'd feel different seeing Anna again after the news of her engagement. He thought he'd feel…angrier. That his fury at her silent rejection of him would burn away any last vestiges of desire and tenderness he'd once felt for her.

Instead, it was as if no time had passed—and

naught had changed. Her soft voice still made his innards turn to porridge. Those dark, deep blue eyes sent ripples of awareness through him. And her sweet curves ignited a familiar fire in his veins.

Bloody hell, this was going to be the longest five days of his life.

Chapter Five

Anna tried counting backward from one hundred. She tried envisioning sheep lazily walking across a Highland field. She tried slowing her breath, rolling onto one side and then the other, but naught worked.

When the inside of the wagon began to lighten with approaching dawn, she gave up on sleep altogether, for soon enough the man who'd been haunting her thoughts would be before her in actuality.

Part of her longed to lay eyes on Graeme, this time in the light of day rather than in twilight's gloom. But another part of her dreaded it, for even their brief encounter last night had left her in shambles.

He was so dreadfully handsome. Aye, he was rough around the edges, but that only made him more alluring in her eyes. Last night, his sandy blond hair had been pulled back in its usual loose and messy queue at the base of his neck. He'd worn several days' worth of scruff on his jaw, and his simple woolen cloak had looked rumpled with travel, as had his linen tunic and blue and green MacKay plaid.

With one lopsided grin, he could have set her knees to trembling, but instead, he'd been cold and harsh with her.

She couldn't blame him. He knew not what was in her heart, nor what role her father had played in ending their communication and arranging for her engagement to Laird Munro.

A sliver of her—the foolish, silly, romantic girl that still lived in her heart—had hoped against hope that when the banns announcing her engagement to Laird Munro had been read, Graeme would come charging into the Highlands, demanding that the marriage be called off.

Even more ridiculously, she'd let herself imagine that he would sweep her away from the Ross keep and wed her himself. Kidnapping one's bride wasn't so preposterous an event in the Highlands. A wedding was a wedding, and Anna would take a kidnapping and a forbidden marriage that went against her father's wishes if it meant she could marry Graeme.

Or so she had fancied, but those were the

musings of a silly lass. In reality, Graeme hadn't come riding to the Ross clan's castle gates, demanding her and her alone. In reality, she'd acquiesced to her arranged marriage with Laird Munro, for it was best for her people. And in reality, Graeme now hated her for it.

Though it wouldn't change aught, she at least owed him an explanation. Aye, she would still marry Laird Munro, for her clan was counting on this alliance. But if naught else, Graeme would know what was in her heart—that she loved him and had tried to accept his proposal.

Anna sat up and straightened her dress, making sure the two folded pieces of parchment were still in place over her heart. She quickly plaited her hair and pinched her cheeks to chase away the fatigue from a sleepless night. Then there was naught left to do but face the day—and Graeme.

Just as she pulled back the wagon's flap, the patter of raindrops began to rustle the leaves and drum against the canvas.

The men of her retinue had apparently already begun to rise for the day, but as the rain rapidly grew heavier, they moved swiftly to break camp and saddle their horses.

She caught sight of Graeme's blue and green plaid in the sea of red wool.

"Graeme," she called over the increasingly loud rainfall.

He turned his emerald gaze on her, and she noticed that his eyes were tight with strain and shadowed with fatigue. Mayhap sleep had evaded him as well.

She opened her mouth to call him over in the hopes that they could catch a moment of privacy and she could explain things. Even before she could form the words, however, Graeme ducked his head against the rain and hurried on with his tasks, limping slightly.

Just then, Jerome stepped into her line of sight, cutting off her view of Graeme.

"Ye'd best ready yerself for the day's travels, my lady," Jerome said curtly. "This rain will only slow us down further. We'll have a long day ahead."

Barely repressing a shudder at the thought of not only another grueling, bumpy journey, but a wet one as well, Anna nodded.

It seemed as though she would be forced to wait to speak with Graeme.

ANNA LET her body sway with the motion of the wagon. The hammer of the rain against the canvas roof was nigh deafening, but at least she was dry inside.

It had rained nonstop all morning and through their brief midday break to rest the animals and take a small meal. Now that they'd resumed the trek, she knew the men were soaking wet and likely miserable atop their horses.

Suddenly, the wagon lurched sharply to the left. There was a loud snap and a rough jolt, and the back left corner of the wagon abruptly dropped downward by a foot.

A startled cry rose in Anna's throat as she was tossed against the side of the wagon roughly.

"Shite!" someone snapped beyond the wagon's canvas covering.

Anna righted herself and drew back one of the makeshift canvas window coverings. Hesitantly, she stuck her head out into the driving rain.

"Is all well?"

From the look on the face of the man sitting on the bench at the front of the wagon, it wasn't. He peered back through the downpour at the left rear wheel. Anna followed his gaze.

Not only was the wheel deeply submerged in an enormous mud- and water-filled crater in the path, but the wheel had snapped and crumpled in half, leaving it more an oval than a circle.

"What happened?" Jerome barked, reining his horse around.

"I couldnae see the hole, what with all the mud and rain," the wagon's driver said apologetically.

Jerome muttered a curse. He glanced around at the other guards who were waiting for his order.

"If all the men put their shoulder to the back of the wagon, we could no doubt get it out of that hole," Jerome said, frowning.

Graeme pulled his horse to a halt next to Jerome. "Aye, but we wouldnae be able to fix that broken wheel."

Jerome glared darkly at Graeme, but Graeme was right from what Anna could see.

Breathing another curse, Jerome seemed to make up his mind. "We'll leave the wagon behind. Dennis, ye and Keith share Keith's horse and ride back the way we came."

Dennis, the driver of the wagon, mumbled discontentedly as he began to lower himself from the bench.

Keith, one of the younger guards, urged his horse forward. "Where are we to go?" He looked about at pleased as Dennis at the prospect of having to stay behind.

"An hour's ride the way we came, there was a turn-off to Stirling," Jerome replied. "Find someone who can repair the wagon and bring him to it. Then ye'll take the wagon back to Laird Ross."

"We could simply wait for a new wheel to be brought from Stirling," Graeme said, his shoulders hunched in his cloak against the heavy rain.

"Nay," Jerome snapped. "Laird Munro expects his bride to arrive a sennight after the final banns were read. It is my responsibility to see it done. I'll no' fail him."

"And it is *my* responsibility to ensure Anna's safety and wellbeing," Graeme said tightly. "I'm sure yer Laird wouldnae want her traveling in these conditions."

"We are sitting ducks for bandits and thieves out here," Jerome shot back. "We cannae stay with the wagon. We must keep moving."

Even from several paces away and through a curtain of rain, Anna could see Graeme's jaw muscles twitch. "And how do ye propose that Lady Anna travel without the use of the wagon?"

Jerome thought for a moment. "Mayhap we can unhitch the mules from the wagon and she can ride one of those."

Anna sucked in a breath. Graeme's gaze darted to her before he leveled Jerome with a hard stare. "Ye'd have the future wife of yer Laird ride a mule. Without a saddle. Or a bridle. Through a storm."

Jerome let out a frustrated noise. "Since ye seem to ken what *no'* to do, what would ye suggest?"

Graeme scrubbed a hand over his dripping, stubble-covered chin. After a long moment, he exhaled. His gaze rose to Anna, and a jolt of awareness shot through her.

"She can ride with me."

Anna gasped again, and Jerome shook his head sternly.

"Nay. One of the men can double up with someone, and she can have her own horse."

Anna's stomach knotted tight at the thought. She'd have to sit atop one of the enormous war horses the guards rode, by herself, and try to control such a large animal?

"Anna doesnae feel comfortable with horses," Graeme said evenly before Anna could form an excuse that would save her from having to ride by herself.

He remembered. Warmth filled her chest at the realization that he not only recalled her discomfort around horses, but that he was trying to protect her from a frightening experience.

"It isnae...*appropriate* for Lady Anna to ride with ye," Jerome said through clenched teeth.

"She has to ride with someone," Graeme fired back.

Jerome opened his mouth to reply, but sensing that the disagreement was reaching its boiling point, Anna dove into the conversation.

"It is all right, Jerome. As Graeme says, I am no' a strong rider. It would be best for me to ride with someone." She pulled in a breath, steeling herself for the next words. They would hurt Graeme, but at least they would soothe Jerome's wariness. "It might as well be Graeme. I am engaged to Laird Munro now, and riding with a man—*any* man—doesnae threaten or change that."

Her gaze sought Graeme, and just as she feared, he flinched slightly, his bright green eyes darkening and his jaw locking.

"Verra well," Jerome muttered, pulling her attention back to him.

Anna dropped the canvas flap and brought her head back into the shelter of the covered wagon. She glanced at the large wooden trunk at the other end. She would have to leave it here.

Thankfully, she hadn't packed all her worldly possessions, as she'd expected to return to the Highlands not long after her wedding. She'd planned on sending for the majority of her clothes and keepsakes once she got settled on Munro land. Still, she wouldn't be able to take the fine gown she'd planned to wear for her wedding.

Anna dug out a stout, plain cloak from the trunk and, after tucking a few of her most essential personal items into the cloak's pockets, she drew back the canvas covering at the back of the wagon.

The ground looked very far away all of a sudden—and very muddy. She lowered herself to a seat on the edge of the wagon, stretching her toes toward the wet, churned path.

Just then she heard a grunt nearby and looked up. The other men still sat in their saddles, hunched against the rain—except for Graeme. He'd dismounted and was striding toward her, his limp pronounced.

Without a word, he scooped her into his arms and lifted her out of the wagon.

Inhaling in surprise, Anna's arms looped around Graeme's neck and her fingers sank into the wet wool over his shoulders. He moved slowly, and she could feel from the tension in his neck that he was fighting against his limp. Yet she did not fear that he would drop her, for his arms were strong and solid around her.

When they reached his waiting horse, he lifted her fully onto the animal's back. With a soft grunt, he swung into the saddle behind her, settling her across his lap.

As the retinue, minus Dennis, Keith, and Anna's wagon, began its journey southward once more, Graeme leaned close to her ear.

"Nervous?" His low voice sent a shiver down her spine.

Anna suddenly realized that her lips were pulled into a trembling smile.

"A-aye," she murmured. "Because of the horse."

In truth, she'd hardly noticed the huge bay steed beneath her, for all she seemed to be able to take in at the moment was Graeme.

His powerful thighs beneath her bottom.

His strong arms looped around her, holding her close.

His solid, warm torso, which bumped into her

side with each of the horse's steps.

"Graeme," she said softly, looking up at him through the heavy rain.

His gaze dropped to hers, and behind his stone-hard green eyes, she saw a flicker of uncertainty. Of hurt. "Aye?"

"I…I need to explain myself," she murmured. "This isnae what ye think."

"Isnae it?" She saw his gaze flatten and sensed that her opportunity was slipping away.

"Nay," she insisted, holding his stare. "Please, just hear me out. I ken I cannae change my fate now, or yers, but at least let me explain."

A crack formed in his hard features as he searched her face. "Verra well," he murmured at last. "But as ye say, it willnae change aught."

Even as her heart sank at his cold tone, hope budded there as well. Aye, she may not be able to heal the wounds between them completely, but at least he would understand what had happened after she'd received his missive.

Just as she opened her mouth to explain, Jerome reined his horse from the front of the retinue to the middle where Anna rode with Graeme. Without a word, Jerome guided his horse alongside theirs, casting them a glance out of the corner of his eye.

It appeared as though Jerome planned to monitor them for the entire ride.

"Later," Graeme said, so softly that it was barely a breath against her ear.

She tilted her head in a single nod, then turned her gaze ahead to the muddy, forested road ahead, praying for time to fly until she had an opportunity to speak with Graeme—alone.

Chapter Six

Graeme sent up a silent prayer for time to slow to a halt.

This moment was perfect. He only wished he was lucky enough for it to last forever.

Anna was in his arms, her sweet scent drifting all around him even through the driving rain. Her soft curves pressed into him in all the right places. Hell, he didn't even notice the dull ache in his right thigh beneath the lushness of her bottom.

Just as he'd noted upon first laying eyes on her in the wagon, she was still as beautiful as he remembered. But now that he was this close to her, there were so many things his memory had glossed over since last he'd seen her.

He'd forgotten how much he loved that pert little nose of hers, and the gentle point to her delicate chin. He knew her smile was from nerves and not genuine happiness at being in his embrace, but poor fool that he was, he would take it and be grateful all the same, for she never looked prettier than when her pink lips curved and her cheeks flushed rosily.

He hadn't seen her since March, nearly four months past. He'd been traveling from the Highlands to the Lowlands, for his cousin Colin had urged him to join the Bruce's siege on Berwick castle that was to take place in April. He'd stolen a kiss from Anna before he'd left, assuring her that he would write as soon as the siege was over to confirm that he was well.

But then that bloody arrow had pierced his thigh, and the fever and his slow recovery had laid him low.

It had been May before he'd written to her, eager despite his scar and limp to spread his heart at her feet and claim her as his bride.

And then he'd gotten a month and a half of silence, followed by the announcement of her engagement.

Graeme shoved the dark thoughts aside, trying to cling a little longer to this perfect moment with Anna.

Soon enough, they'd stop for the night, and then she would explain all the reasons she didn't want him anymore—the injury that made him limp, the unsightly scar that she would no doubt be repulsed by, his lack of position within his clan, the fact that he was a MacKay instead of a Munro, and on and on.

Afterward, his final delusions that there was still something between them would be good and crushed. But until then, she was soft and warm in his arms. The tail end of her golden plait poked out from beneath her cloak's hood, brushing against his arm. She'd leaned back against him a few hours past, her head resting on his shoulder.

God, why couldn't this ride last forever?

But all too quickly, the gray, stormy sky overhead began to darken to lead, then charcoal.

Next to them, Jerome spurred his horse to the front of the group and threw up a fist, signaling that they would stop for the night.

When they drew their animals to a halt a little way off the path, Jerome dismounted and went to Graeme's horse. He brusquely lifted Anna down from Graeme's arms and guided her by the elbow under a large tree that provided shelter from the rain.

Graeme dismounted slowly, suddenly feeling all the aches and pains from so many long hours in the saddle. In silence, he and the others tended to their horses, then began to make a rudimentary camp. They built a fire in front of the tree under which Anna stood and began passing around old biscuits and dried venison.

"Even with the wagon slowing us down those first few days," Jerome said once the men were settled, "we can move faster now that we are all on horseback."

Jerome's gaze flicked to Anna, and Graeme felt his jaw tighten. He thought *he* was blunt to the point of being rude, but Jerome far outdid him when it came to ignoring tact in favor of directness.

"I'd estimate we are only three days from Sweetheart Abbey," Jerome went on. "Laird Munro will be pleased."

Graeme stiffened. "Sweetheart Abbey?" he blurted without thinking. "I thought we were going to Lochmaben."

Jerome turned cool eyes on Graeme. "Laird Munro wishes for the ceremony to take place as soon as Lady Anna arrives. He instructed me to escort her directly to Sweetheart Abbey, no' far from Lochmaben, so that he could easily go directly from his meetings with the King to his wedding."

Shite. Graeme hadn't realized he was literally delivering Anna straight to her wedding—and into the arms of another man. For some reason he thought he'd have more time if he was taking her to Lochmaben instead.

But more time for what? He silently berated himself for his foolishness. It wasn't as if he could stop the wedding, or convince her not to go through with it. She didn't want him. In fact, she was about to tell him as much, if he could figure out a way to get a moment alone with her.

As the others settled around the fire, Graeme's gaze kept tugging to Anna, who stood with her arms wrapped around herself as she stared into the flames. Yet he felt Jerome's hard eyes on him, no doubt watching to ensure that Graeme didn't try to get closer to Anna.

But even Jerome had to heed nature's call eventually. As the other men began wrapping themselves in their plaids and hunkering down against the wet ground, Jerome rose and made his way into the underbrush for privacy.

Steeling himself with a breath, Graeme stalked around the fire until he stood before Anna. As Colin had said, it was best to get this over with once and for all. Then mayhap the hole in his heart could begin to heal.

"Well, lass," he said, his voice coming out gruff. "Ye wished to say yer piece, so have at it."

She looked up at him and their gazes locked. Suddenly he was drowning in the perfect blue of her eyes. They swallowed him like a deep Highland loch, and all at once he felt like he might as well be trying to breathe underwater.

"I tried to write back to ye," she blurted. "But my father wouldnae let me send my missive. He told everyone in the keep no' to help me deliver it."

Her hand fluttered up to her heart in the same

gesture she'd first made when he'd yanked back the canvas on the wagon.

Graeme felt his brows lower. Why would Laird Ross forbid her from sending a response to his missive? Unless…unless the Laird knew what was in Anna's heart but could not allow it for the sake of the clan.

His heart suddenly leapt against his ribs, but Graeme would not let himself hope. Not yet, anyway.

"Why wouldnae he let ye respond?" he asked cautiously.

"Because the very day yer missive arrived, he informed me that he wished to begin talks with Laird Munro about a marriage alliance between our clans."

So she hadn't been repulsed by the thought of his injured leg, or the fact that he was less of a warrior now that he would likely bear a limp for the rest of his life. The air whooshed from Graeme's lungs.

Nay, he was jumping ahead of himself. She hadn't said what her answer to his proposal would have been.

"My father told me that our courtship had to end for the good of the clan. He said it was my duty to our people to secure this alliance with the Munros. He believed that if I wrote to ye, it would only make matters more painful for both of us, and that it would be a kindness to ye to cut things off cleanly."

Graeme hardly thought leaving a marriage proposal unanswered was considered a clean break, but then again, a new realization struck. Mayhap Laird Ross hadn't known the contents of Graeme's missive, in which case, he wouldn't have been aware of Graeme's proposal.

Graeme had always gotten the impression that Laird Ross had tolerated Graeme's courtship of Anna because he thought it little more than an innocent dalliance. It seemed he'd already decided that his only daughter could never marry a MacKay, but until such time as he arranged her marriage alliance, Laird Ross could be permitted to indulge his beloved child's happiness.

But it had always been so much more than that to Graeme.

From the moment he'd laid eyes on her at a Highland fair two years past, he'd known Anna was the only lass for him. He'd nearly killed himself during the caber toss and hammer throwing events in an attempt to catch her eye. And when she'd finally noticed him, he'd kissed her hand and vowed to remain at her side for the rest of the festivities.

And he had. A fortnight later, when the fair ended and the various clans scattered to their corners of the Highlands once more, he'd kissed her, this time on her sweet mouth, and promised to send her missives regularly, and visit when he could.

As a warrior in Robert the Bruce's army, his time was usually not his own, but whenever he was in the Highlands, or passing by the Ross keep on his way to the Lowlands, the two met for as long as they could spare.

Even before his injury had made him realize the depth of his love for Anna, he had always planned to propose to her, clan tensions and his own lack of position and power be damned. When two people loved each other so deeply, he'd believed, all that could be overcome.

He'd been wrong, of course. Even if Anna was now telling him what his heart longed to hear—that she'd still wanted him after receiving the news of his injury, that it had been her father and not her who had wished for the union with Laird Munro—as she had said, it changed naught.

Who was Graeme to destroy an alliance between two powerful Highland Lairds, especially at such a delicate and important time for Robert the Bruce's mission to unite all of Scotland against England?

"Mayhap yer father was right," Graeme said wearily. "Mayhap it is better this way. We couldnae be together, no' with our clans so uneasy with each other."

Anna's eyes clouded with tears, but she did not

break their gaze. "I ken that," she said, her voice tight with emotion. "But I still believe ye have a right to hear the truth. I still love ye, Graeme MacKay. I never stopped."

Graeme's breath stuck in his throat as he gazed down at her. It was everything he'd ever wanted to hear, and yet it felt as though his heart was being torn in two for the second time in as many months. What good was love when he was forbidden from seizing it?

"I did write back to ye," she breathed, once again bringing her hand to her heart. He thought he heard the faint crinkle of parchment, but he couldn't make sense of why the noise would be coming from the bodice of her dress.

"Even though my father wouldnae let me send it, I replied to yer proposal," she went on, her eyes holding him transfixed. "My answer was—"

Just then a rustling off to the right had Graeme's head whipping around. Without thinking, he put himself in front of Anna, using his body to shield her.

"Is that ye, Jerome?" Graeme said loudly, causing some of the guards to stir from their rest.

"Nay." Jerome stepped from the underbrush a stone's throw farther to the right than the noise. He looked around warily, for he must have heard the rustling as well.

Another soft rasp of leaves and branches

sounded to the left. Just as a knot of dread tightened in Graeme's stomach, Jerome's eyes widened.

"Ambush!" Jerome bellowed, yanking his sword free of the sheath on his hip.

The guards sprang from the ground at the same moment that more than a dozen men burst from the trees surrounding them, weapons already bared. The Munros and Rosses barely had time to draw their swords before their attackers fell upon them. The night air exploded with metallic clangs and battle cries.

Graeme jerked his sword from its sheath, wrapping one arm behind him to hold Anna to his back.

"Stay close!" he roared over the sudden cacophony of battle.

Graeme met an oncoming ambusher, blocking the man's blade from cleaving him in two. He sidestepped but fumbled as his weight came down on his bad leg.

Barely regaining his footing before his attacker's blade could pierce his flesh, he blocked again, then turned the defensive maneuver into an attack. He slid his blade along his enemy's, binding it with a twist of his wrist so that he deflected the point of his opponent's weapon away from him and drove his sword into the man's chest.

With a scream, the man crumpled to the forest floor, but as soon as he fell, another bandit took his place.

Graeme backed up, pushing Anna backward and trying to buy himself time. His leg screamed in protest at him, making his steps sluggish and awkward. His new attacker's eyes dropped to Graeme's right leg as if realizing Graeme's weakness and his own advantage. A slow smile curled the man's lips as he advanced on Graeme.

Nay.

Graeme's stomach spiked with hot panic.

Because of his injury, he would not be able to protect Anna.

His greatest fear had come true.

Chapter Seven

Holding his sword before them both, Graeme reached back and grabbed Anna by the arm. He shoved her hard.

"Get to my horse!" he shouted above the fray.

Anna's mind was so flooded with fear that she could do naught but obey. She bolted to where the animals were tethered in the trees. The horses sidestepped wildly, their eyes rolling and their ears pulling back as the battle raged all around.

A new terror washed over her as she approached Graeme's bay. What if she were trampled to death by the frightened beasts?

"Saddle and bridle him!" Graeme's voice sliced through her panic. He was still backing up toward her, deflecting his attacker's blows with his sword. As he shoved his opponent away, he darted a glance at her over his shoulder. "Now, Anna!"

There was no time to hesitate, no time to let her fears take over.

She grabbed the nearest saddle and hefted it up with a grunt. She was barely able to hoist it over the enormous bay's high back, but the fear surging in her veins gave her added strength. With a nonsensical murmured word to soothe the horse, she bent and buckled the saddle under its belly.

The clang of Graeme's sword against his enemy's was growing louder. As Anna fumbled with the bridle, she dared a look in his direction. He was only a few paces away now, though he seemed to be fighting on his heels, defensively batting away his attacker's advances.

Fingers trembling, Anna secured the bridle on the horse's head and looped the reins over his neck.

With a sudden surge of strength and speed, Graeme went on the offensive, slashing out against his enemy. In two strokes, he'd overpowered the bandit, delivering a deadly slice across the man's neck.

Graeme spun and bolted toward her as fast as his limp would allow.

"Grab hold of the pommel," he ordered.

Anna wrapped both hands around the saddle's pommel. One of Graeme's big, rough palms was suddenly under her bottom, pushing her with great force up and onto the saddle.

His sword still drawn and dripping with blood, Graeme swung up behind her.

"MacKay!" Jerome's bellow cut through the chaos and roar of the battle.

Anna's gaze landed on Jerome, who stood in the middle of the melee. He, too, held a bloodied sword, and several of the bandits' bodies lay sprawled around him.

To her relief, Anna noticed that her Munro and Ross guards were all still standing, whereas their attackers' numbers were beginning to thin.

"What the bloody hell are ye doing, MacKay?" Jerome shouted, his dark eyes blazing with fury.

"I'm getting her out of here—to safety!" Graeme barked back.

With no further hesitation, she felt Graeme's legs squeeze into the horse's flanks. He slapped the reins with one hand, still brandishing his sword in case any of the bandits attacked them as they fled.

The bay surged forward, eager to escape the noise and turmoil of the skirmish.

Anna clung tightly to the pommel as the night-darkened forest blurred around them and they sped onward. Her heart hammered in time with the horse's pounding hooves, but as they drew farther from the melee, her fear drained away. Graeme was warm and solid behind her. She knew in her very bones that he would never let any harm befall her.

Time seemed to bend as the horse galloped on

through the shadowed woods. She had no idea how long they'd been riding, but it must have been a long while, for when Graeme reined in the bay, the animal's flanks rose and fell rapidly with his hard breathing.

Anna realized with a start that sometime during their wild flight, the fierce summer storm had ebbed. Only a light misting drizzle lingered in the air.

With a grunt of pain, Graeme dismounted behind her. He wiped his bloodied blade on the rain-dampened moss and re-sheathed it at last.

"I think we lost them," he said. His voice sounded unnaturally loud in the quiet forest, whose only sounds were the horse's breathing and the muted whisper of the soft rain in the trees.

"Wh-who were those men?" Anna asked.

"Bandits, most likely," Graeme replied. "They wore no clan colors, and if they had succeeded with their surprise attack, they probably would have happily gutted us all and taken aught of value they could." Graeme's gaze scanned the forest around them. "In these times of war, men grow desperate—and overconfident. Some seek to capitalize on the chaos that war brings by attacking supply convoys or even soldiers who are equipped by the King."

"Why?" Anna asked, shaking her head in confusion. "We are all Scots, arenae we? Why would those bandits seek to harm and steal from their own?"

Graeme's gaze lifted to hers. "Aye, we are all Scots, but that hasnae stopped us from unending infighting. Just look at our clans. The MacKays and Rosses have no true quarrel, but our alliances and feuds with other clans means that we cannae—"

He cut off sharply, and Anna wondered what his next words would have been. Was he only thinking of the fact that their clans couldn't seem to get along, or that the two of them couldn't be together?

Graeme cleared his throat. "A few desperate or greedy men will always try to prey on others. Thank God we were no' all asleep when they struck, else we may no' have made it out alive."

Anna swallowed. "Aye. From what I saw just before we fled, it looked as though the Rosses and Munros had the upper hand."

Graeme nodded, then moved beside the horse to mount once more. "I saw that too. We'd best make our way back to them. Jerome will have my hide for riding off with ye, but I could think of no other way to keep ye safe."

He paused, his right foot in the stirrup and his left supporting all his weight. His hand dropped to his right thigh and massaged it for a moment. "Damned cursed leg," he muttered.

Sadness and shame washed through Anna—

sadness for all that Graeme had been through, and shame that he assumed she would love him any less over an injury he'd earned serving their King. There was so much more to explain. Her heart ached with the need to reassure him that his wound meant naught to her.

"Stop," she said just before he boosted himself into the saddle.

He froze, looking up at her, his eyes dark and unreadable in the moonless night.

Without waiting for his assistance, she lifted her leg over the bay's neck and slid to the ground with a little grunt.

"What are ye—"

"I need to finish what I started to say," she replied. "Just before the bandits attacked, I told ye I wrote back to ye."

Graeme stilled, his eyes flickering with sadness. "Ye neednae go on, lass. I ken that ye cannae change things now—neither of us can. As I said before, mayhap yer father was right—mayhap it is best to let this die once and for all."

She stared up at him, her throat growing tight. "It matters to me," she managed at last. "If naught else, I need ye to ken the truth of things. It breaks my heart to imagine what ye must have thought, what ye must have been through in the Bruce's camp as ye waited to receive an answer from me."

Graeme let out a long, slow breath. At last, he nodded reluctantly. "Verra well, then."

Taking the horse's reins in one hand and Anna's elbow in the other, he guided them toward two large trees that would provide shelter from the drizzle.

As Graeme tethered the horse under one of the trees, Anna found a dry patch of old pine needles beneath the boughs. The two trees' branches overlapped and wound together like embracing arms, forming a dense bower overhead that completely blocked the rain.

Graeme lowered himself beside her, extending his stiff right leg as he did.

In the misty dimness, her eyes found his and warmth swept through her veins. Her heart hitched, thumping against her ribs. She shouldn't let herself feel so much for him, for her life was not her own anymore. Yet her body responded of its own volition to his nearness.

"Ye cannae know how much yer missive meant to me," she began, her voice barely more than a whisper. "I read it over and over. If the touch of my eyes on the parchment were the same as the touch of a hand, the ink would have been rubbed away by now and the parchment turned to dust. Thank God it was no'."

Anna slid her hand inside her cloak and placed it over her heart. Blessedly, the stout wool had kept the bodice of her gown dry. She pulled Graeme's missive from beneath her shift and began unfolding it.

"Ye...ye kept it?" Graeme murmured, his gaze widening on the square of parchment.

"Aye. I hid it against my heart all this time," she said, the missive trembling in her fingers. "I dinnae even need to read it anymore, for the words are emblazoned on my heart."

Still, she finished unfolding it and extended it toward him to prove her words.

"I wept tears of sorrow to read what ye had been through with yer leg," she said, "and tears of joy when ye laid yer heart bare and asked me to be yer wife."

Slowly, he took the missive from her and scanned it. He let out a ragged breath.

"It feels like a lifetime ago that I wrote these words," he said. He lowered the missive, staring out into the darkened trees. "I was a fool."

The words were softly spoken, but Anna did not miss the bitter edge they held.

"Nay, Graeme, ye werenae."

"Aye, I was. I was a fool to think that love could overcome our clans' dislike of each other, and the fact that yer father wanted the Munro Laird for ye, and...and *this*."

He cast his hand over his extended right leg, his

sandy brows lowered and his mouth pinched into a frown.

She caught his wrist before he'd finished the gesture. "Listen to me, Graeme MacKay, and listen well. I dinnae care a lick what state yer leg is in—or whether ye have legs at all."

His startled gaze met hers. He blinked, then opened his mouth to respond, but she went on before he could form some other reason against her loving him.

"The news of yer injury had naught to do with my engagement to Laird Munro, or the fact that ye never received a missive from me. As I told ye, my father made the arrangements with Laird Munro and forbade me from writing to ye. But that doesnae mean that I didnae try. Or that I loved ye any less because of yer wounded leg—and I can prove it."

She reached into her bodice once more and removed the second missive she kept there.

"Read it," she said, extending the missive toward him.

He took it with a wary glance at her, then unfolded it and smoothed it out on top of his missive to her.

His eyes scanned the words she knew by heart. She'd told him how frightened she'd been at the thought of losing him—not just to the injury, but to anything that threatened to separate them. That feeling of certainty that she never wanted them to be parted, she'd written, made her love him even more deeply. And it was because of that certainty that she could say without hesitation that…

"…Ye accept my proposal to be wed," he said out loud.

"Aye," she replied, her throat tight with emotion. "I accepted ye. There is yer proof that I didnae stop loving ye once I learned of yer injury, or set ye aside unfeelingly when my father arranged for me to wed Laird Munro instead."

Graeme's eyes captured hers, and she saw pain war with love in their green depths.

"Damn it all," he murmured a heartbeat before his arm snaked around her waist and pulled her against his chest.

He dropped his head, and suddenly he was kissing her.

Chapter Eight

Anna's heart leapt wildly as Graeme's mouth claimed hers.

This was not the sweet, playful brush of lips that he used when he was trying to coax a shy smile from her. Nor was it the sad, slow kiss they shared whenever they knew they were saying goodbye for an indefinite number of sennights or months.

Nay, this kiss was like naught Anna had ever experienced before. It was edged with urgency and laced with lust. Judging from the taut rigidity of Graeme's body, he was barely managing to hold his raw power in check as his tongue swept inside her mouth. She yielded to him—to this moment—completely, unable to fight the wave of longing that flooded her.

His hand fisted in the material at the back of her dress, holding her flush against the hard wall of his chest. The scruff on his chin rasped along her skin, but the scrape only heightened her spiraling senses. Through the blood roaring in her ears, she heard him groan desperately. An echoing moan rose in her throat.

Graeme. It had always been Graeme, and it would always be Graeme, no matter who or what came after him. What they shared was too powerful to be ignored, snuffed out, overridden, or forgotten. It was their hearts' destiny to remain locked in this embrace forever.

Graeme pulled back, his breath ragged and his eyes clouded with need as he stared down at her.

But then his blond brows dropped sharply, and his gaze drifted to the forest floor off to the side.

"Ye said, when yer father arranged..." he murmured, repeating her words.

He jerked the two missives, which he still held in one hand, up in front of his gaze, flipping between the two.

"I wrote this missive on the tenth of May, when my fever finally broke and the putrescence had been removed from the flesh surrounding the wound," he said. He pointed to the date scrawled in the corner of the parchment. "I made sure to note the date, for it felt like a second birth to have survived."

She nodded, but felt her brow furrow in uncertainty. "Aye. I received it on the sixteenth. The Bruce's messenger told me he'd traveled with all haste, for he said ye were considered a hero around the Bruce's camp after Berwick," she replied. "He wanted to make sure that yer missive was delivered promptly and directly into my hands."

"And yer missive is dated the seventeenth," Graeme went on, flipping back to the other sheet of parchment. "The verra next day."

"Aye," Anna said again, her confusion deepening. "I wrote it as soon as I could see through my tears. My father informed me the same day yer missive arrived that he would speak to Laird Munro about a marriage alliance."

He reached out and clasped her hand in his, holding her gaze. His eyes were filled with a sudden urgency that made her pulse quicken. "This is verra important, Anna, so I would ask ye to consider before ye speak and be certain of yer answer."

She nodded. "What is it?"

"Had yer father already contacted Laird Munro about a marriage alliance before the seventeenth of May?"

As he requested, she thought carefully, but she knew the answer without a doubt. "Nay."

"How can ye be sure?" he prodded, still holding her hand tight. "Mayhap he sent word by way of the King's messenger on the sixteenth when ye received my missive."

"Nay," she repeated, shaking her head firmly. "He didnae. I watched the King's messenger leave empty-handed that day. My father then came to tell me that he would seek an arranged marriage for me with Laird Munro, hoping that I might find the match agreeable. When I burst into tears at the idea, he asked what was wrong, and I told him of yer proposal. That was when he said I shouldnae respond to ye, for it would only draw out the anguish for both of us."

Anna dragged in a deep breath against the painful memories. "I went against his wishes, though. I wrote to ye the next morning. I learned that my father's own personal messenger was preparing to leave for Munro land to deliver a missive opening negotiations for my marriage to the Laird. I tried to slip my response to ye in with my father's missive, but the messenger informed me that he'd been ordered no' to deliver any letters from me to ye."

"So ye kept yer missive," Graeme finished. "And the messenger departed, no doubt delivering the proposal to Laird Munro a day or two later."

"Aye," Anna said. "But what is this all about? Why does any of it matter?" It pained her to ask, but she couldn't deny reality. She was engaged to Laird Munro now, and her love for Graeme didn't change that.

"Dinnae ye see, lass?" Graeme said, his eyes lighting with green fire. "I asked ye to marry me, and ye accepted. We have the dates to prove it right here." He held up the two missives.

"What are ye saying?" Anna asked slowly.

"That these missives attest to the fact that ye were already engaged when yer father sought to arrange a union with Laird Munro."

He squeezed her hand, an awed smile widening his mouth. "Ye cannae enter into a new engagement when a previous one still stands. Which means ye willnae marry Laird Munro."

Graeme stood suddenly, his leg hardly slowing him down. He pulled her to her feet, holding her gaze. "Ye willnae marry him," he repeated, his voice growing stronger. "For we will be married instead."

Anna felt her mouth fall open. Her heart sang in her chest. Was it true? Was it possible?

Aye, she'd agreed to marry Graeme before the arrangements had been made with Laird Munro. In the eyes of the church, she could not be engaged to two different men at the same time, and the first of the two engagements always took precedence—which meant that the second was void.

Though she hadn't been able to say aye to Graeme in person, it now appeared to be far better that they had their pledges to each other in writing—with dates—for it wouldn't just be their word against her father's or Laird Munro's. They had proof.

"Wh-what...what do we do now?" she gasped, staring at Graeme.

His brows drew together in anxious concentration. "We need to get to a priest before any of this can be undone," he said, his eyes scanning the forest floor in thought as he ruffled the missives gently.

Then he lifted his gaze, locking it with hers. "And then we'll wed before anyone can stop us."

Chapter Nine

Anna shifted in Graeme's lap, and this time he had to clamp his teeth against a groan of pain. Even with her perfect form pressed against him, he could not ignore the ache in his thigh.

He'd pushed them both hard for two long, grueling days—far harder than he would have liked, given Anna's discomfort with riding and his own bad leg.

He didn't dare slow down their pace though. In his mind, obstacles lurked everywhere, waiting to thwart this mad scheme of his.

No doubt Jerome and the others had realized after they'd dispatched the last of the bandits that Graeme and Anna weren't coming back. Though bull-headed, Jerome was also smart and sharp. He'd known right from the beginning not to fully trust Graeme in Anna's presence. The fact that Graeme was now whisking Anna away to marry her was proof enough that Jerome had his wits about him.

They'd had at least a few hours' head start on Jerome and the other guards, but knowing Jerome, he would push the men ruthlessly until he caught up with Graeme.

"Are we almost there?" Anna said, shifting once again in the saddle.

Graeme cursed himself for setting such a punishing pace, but he hoped he would be proven justified.

"Aye," he said, checking their surroundings once more. The forest had begun to look familiar. He knew they weren't far outside of Lochmaben now.

They'd managed to turn a three-day's ride into two in their flight from Jerome, but worse than the man at their heels was what lay ahead of them. When Graeme and Anna had fled from the bandits, they'd ridden hard south. Hoping not to lose any of that time, Graeme had decided that it was best they continue southward, even though it meant heading farther into the Lowlands.

Though Graeme had spent some time in the Lowlands with the Bruce's army, he was unfamiliar with the location of towns and villages—besides Lochmaben. As the Bruce's long-standing headquarters of operation, it was the only place with which Graeme had passing familiarity.

Hoping to lose Jerome from their trail, Graeme

had kept them away from the roads in favor of the forest.

The problem was, Graeme had no idea where to find the nearest priest and was too cautious to leave the shelter of the forest to seek out a village and ask, fearing that it would slow them down and give Jerome a chance to catch up.

So he'd made the risky decision to go to the only church he knew in the Lowlands—Sweetheart Abbey, the very place Anna was meant to wed Laird Munro a day from now.

It was perilous, aye, but Graeme didn't know what else to do besides push them toward the abbey as fast as the bay would take them.

Just then, Graeme made out a flicker of red through the dense green trees. He slowed the horse and approached cautiously.

The Abbey of Dolce Cor—or what the Lowlanders called Sweetheart Abbey—emerged from the foliage. Its soaring tower, columns, and long nave were all built with the same red sandstone, making its name even more fitting. Graeme had never seen it before, but he now understood why the magnificent abbey would be considered fit for a Laird's wedding.

Several white-cowled monks worked in the garden surrounding the abbey. They looked up, wiping sweat from their brows, as Graeme and Anna approached.

Graeme dismounted and tethered the horse, then helped Anna down.

"Still have the missives?" he asked.

She patted the bodice of her dress where she'd tucked away the letters, then gave him a nod.

"Ready?"

"Aye," she said, her wide blue eyes sure and steady.

He took her hand and walked toward the abbey, ignoring the curious stares of the monks.

When they reached the high, arching doorway, Graeme pulled open the wooden door and stepped inside with Anna.

"Can I help ye with something, my son?" A priest glided down the nave toward them. He wore the same white cowl that the others had over his simple brown habit, and his tonsured head was bowed slightly toward them.

"Aye, Father," Graeme said, but then he faltered. How could he explain everything that had happened in the last few months—let alone the last few days?

"We are here to be married," Anna said, straightening beside him. Graeme couldn't help but smile at her pluck.

"Ah," the priest said, a knowing look coming into his warm brown eyes. "I understand ye must be eager, young as ye are, to begin yer life as man and wife, but we must read the banns first to ensure that no one can object. There is a proper way to do things, and—"

"Nay, Father," Graeme cut in. "I'm afraid it's a bit more complicated than that."

As Graeme began to explain, Anna removed the two missives from her bodice and held them out to the priest. The priest listened, his gray-brown brows drawing tighter and tighter together as Anna and Graeme described their unusual engagement, Anna's arranged marriage, and their present urgency to not only confirm that their engagement took precedence, but that they could be married swiftly to ensure that their union could not be challenged.

When they came to the end of their tale, the priest looked up from the missives and fixed them with a matter-of-fact look.

"Have ye…ah…indulged in the Godly union of yer bodies?"

Graeme blinked. He glanced at Anna, who was turning redder than the sandstones surrounding them.

"Nay, Father," she squeaked. "We havenae." She darted a glance at Graeme. "We had always planned to wait until our union could be made official."

The priest frowned. "That is unfortunate."

"Beg yer pardon, Father?" Graeme choked out.

Now it was the priest's turn to redden. "Ye see,

it is far easier for the church to recognize these... er...unconventional betrothals when more than one condition is met. Each of ye agreeing to marry and pledging yerselves to each other is one such condition." He held up the missives. "Which ye've met—in writing, no less. Another would be to...ahem... seal the union physically. Since ye havenae done that, it may make things more difficult."

The priest cleared his throat, visibly attempting to regain some of his pious composure.

"I do think there is a chance that this engagement could stand, however," he went on. "If it did, it would void yer later engagement, child," he said, turning to Anna.

"Then ye can wed us now, Father," Graeme urged.

The priest held up a staying hand. "No' quite, my son. Since this engagement was formed in secret, the banns must be read so that it can be made public. All will go far smoother in the long run if any objections are brought forth *before* ye are wed."

"But we have already been engaged for two months according to the dates on the missives," Anna offered. "Doesnae that count for something?"

"I'm sorry, my children," the priest replied. "But as I said, there is a proper way to go about this, and I must follow that course."

Graeme clenched his teeth in frustration, trying

to smother his rising anxiety. "I dinnae think I was clear on just how urgent this is," he said, fighting to keep his tone in check. "Ye see, the lass's fiancé could arrive at any—"

"Halt!"

The abbey's wooden doors banged against the stone walls and sunlight flooded in.

Jerome stood silhouetted in the arched doorway.

And beside him strode a graying man wearing Munro colors who could be none other than—

"I am Laird Munro," the man boomed. "And I demand ye unhand my bride."

Chapter Ten

Anna stared in horror as Laird Donald Munro and Jerome marched down the nave toward them. In the doorway behind the Laird and his commander, Anna could see more than two dozen armed Munro warriors.

They could not flee from this, and they certainly couldn't fight their way out.

But as Laird Munro and Jerome closed the distance between themselves and Graeme, Anna knew she had to do something.

Laird Munro was clearly furious. His graying hair flew wildly from its queue, and his dark eyes blazed with fury. But Anna knew him to be a collected, fair, and honorable man under less chaotic circumstances. He would not hurt her.

However, she could not be sure that the Laird's equity would extend to Graeme at the moment.

Without thinking, Anna stepped in front of Graeme, shielding his body from Laird Munro and Jerome with her own.

"Step aside, Lady Anna," Jerome growled, reaching for the sword at his hip. "Else ye be harmed by this kidnapping scoundrel of a MacKay again."

"Anna, nay," Graeme said, ignoring Jerome as he tried to move around her.

Anna planted a hand in the middle of Graeme's chest to stay him, even though she knew he could easily lift her out of the way if he chose.

"Hold there!" the priest shouted frantically, waving both hands. He, too, stepped between Graeme and the two approaching Munros. "This is a holy house! Ye will no' shed blood here, let alone draw weapons or speak such words of aggression!"

"He didnae kidnap me," Anna said, facing Jerome. "And he is no' a scoundrel—he is my betrothed."

"What the bloody hell is going on here?" Laird Munro demanded, coming to a halt. He turned to the priest. "My apologies, Father, but I will have answers, and I will have them now."

Anna dragged in a breath to explain everything, but before she could speak, Jerome launched in, his hard gaze fixed on Graeme.

"When ye two didnae return after the attack by those bandits, I kenned my suspicions had been right all along," he said. "Ye wanted my Laird's intended for yerself, MacKay."

"How did ye find us?" Graeme ground out behind her.

"When we picked up yer trail headed southward, I figured ye'd come here. I didnae miss the way ye took particular notice of the name of the abbey where my Laird was to wed Lady Anna," Jerome shot back, his eyes filled with dark fury. "Besides, I ken ye've spent time in Lochmaben. I'm no' surprised ye slithered back to someplace familiar, just like the vermin ye are."

She sensed Graeme stiffen behind her, but Jerome went on before he could respond. "As soon as I realized what ye were up to, I went straight to Lochmaben and told Laird Munro what ye were about. Ye'll no' get away this time, MacKay—no' with Anna, and no' with yer life."

"I went willingly!"

Anna hadn't meant to shout, but she couldn't stand any more of Jerome's acid words, nor the accusations being hurled about the church.

Her voice echoed around the abbey's arched ceiling until everyone at last fell silent.

"What is the meaning of all this?" Laird Munro said, his clear struggle to remain calm making his voice low and tight. "What do ye mean ye are his betrothed, Anna?"

Anna sucked in a breath, and for the second

time that hour she explained all that had passed between her and Graeme—their courtship, his proposal, his sudden appearance on her journey to the Lowlands, her missive, their flight—all the way up to this moment.

As she spoke, Laird Munro stood silently, his dark brown eyes unreadable. Jerome's state of mind, however, was written clearly on his hard features. He seethed with barely contained rage, shooting daggers at Graeme with his eyes. His hand still rested on the sheathed sword at his hip despite the priest's plea to respect the sanctity of the abbey.

When Anna concluded her story, the priest cleared his throat.

"I can confirm, Laird Munro, that the missives in question appear to be valid. Lady Anna Ross was already technically engaged before she entered the marriage agreement with ye."

Laird Munro's gaze landed on Anna. She flinched instinctively, but when she met his eyes, she found a surprising gentleness in them.

"And this is what ye want, Anna?" he asked quietly. "To marry this MacKay?"

Anna turned and locked gazes with Graeme.

"Aye, Laird," she said, her voice soft but steady. "It is all I've ever wanted."

Laird Munro let out a slow breath. "Then it appears I cannae stop ye."

Jerome squared his shoulders to Graeme. "Ye've

destroyed an alliance between the Rosses and the Munros today, MacKay—and ye've made two more enemies for yer clan as well. Without this alliance, ye've thrown the Highlands into even more turmoil, ye—"

To Anna's surprise, Laird Munro held up a hand, and Jerome fell instantly silent, his teeth clicking together as he clamped his jaw shut.

"Enough, Jerome," Laird Munro said quietly. He turned to Graeme. "Forgive my commander's sharp tongue. He's the most loyal man ye'll ever meet. I'm most grateful to have earned such faithful devotion—and no' to have ever landed on his bad side."

Jerome still scowled fiercely at Graeme, but in the face of an order from his Laird, he seemed obliged to remain silent.

Still, something he'd said troubled Anna. Jerome was right. If she married Graeme, not only would it dissolve the carefully crafted alliance her father and Laird Munro had forged for their two clans, but it would bring already simmering tensions between the Munros, Rosses, and MacKays to a full-on boil.

Anna had agreed to wed Laird Munro solely for their clans' benefit. She'd always known it would be her duty as the daughter of a Laird to form an alliance through marriage. What of her duty now?

How could she follow her heart toward Graeme if it meant endangering her people?

She looked up at Graeme, sinking her teeth into her lower lip. From the cloud of unease that crossed his green eyes, he'd had the same thought.

"What does this mean for our people?" Anna asked softly.

Laird Munro sighed, drawing her attention back to him.

"I'll speak with yer father," he said, suddenly sounding weary. "The Munros and Rosses have a great deal of good blood between them. Surely with time there will be a way to smooth this over."

"And the MacKays?" Graeme murmured. "Will this pit my clan against no' only the Rosses, but the Munros as well?"

Laird Munro exhaled again, dragging a hand through his disheveled gray-brown hair. "We all want peace," he said. "But it is hard to come by in the Highlands, it seems."

Anna felt Graeme stiffen behind her. She turned to find him staring intently at Laird Munro.

"What is it?" she whispered.

Brows drawn together and face set in stone, he looked every bit the fierce warrior she'd fallen in love with, but she could also see the intricate wheels of his mind working behind his bright green eyes.

"I have an idea."

Chapter Eleven

By the time the priest had guided them all to a private chamber set back from the nave and they'd been seated around a small circular table, anxiety gnawed viciously in Anna's stomach.

What could Graeme possibly have in mind? His knee brushed hers beneath the table and he gave her a reassuring look before turning his attention to Laird Munro and Jerome.

"As ye said, Laird Munro, the alliance between yer clan and the Rosses has long been stable," he began.

"Aye," Laird Munro said cautiously. "Though in uncertain times like these, an alliance can never be too strong."

"Yer main concern is the Mackenzies, is it no'?" Graeme went on. "Both ye and the Rosses share a border with them, and they are a large and powerful clan."

Laird Munro nodded once, his brows drawn together.

"The MacKays have lands that border the Mackenzies as well," Graeme said. "But we worry less about them because of our alliance with the Sutherlands."

"And the Rosses dinnae like the Sutherlands, so the Rosses dinnae like the MacKays, and therefore the Munros, who like the Rosses, dinnae like the MacKays either, and on and on," Laird Munro finished, a frown on his face. "I ken all this, lad. What is yer point?"

Graeme leaned forward, propping his elbows on the little wooden table. "My point is, Laird, we are all Highlanders united behind Robert the Bruce and the cause for freedom."

He turned to Anna and surprised her by taking her hand. "Anna reminded me of that," he said, his gaze soft on her for a moment before he went on. "We've come together before—to join our forces for the Bruce's cause. Is it no' madness that we should continue this endless clan squabbling when we have been fighting and dying alongside one another on the battlefield against the English?"

Graeme's attention shifted to Jerome. "Just this past April, I was part of the King's siege on Berwick

Castle. I fought alongside a Munro. When I took an arrow to the leg, he dragged me to cover. If it wasnae for him, I'd have been turned into a MacKay pin-pillow by the English archers, and my bones would be buried outside Berwick's wall right now."

Anna's hand tightened on Graeme's as he continued. "I also fought beside a Sutherland, and a Ross, and a Mackenzie, as well as a MacLeod and other MacKays. Dinnae ye see? We are on the same side for once in our bloody lives. This in-fighting needs to stop before we make complete arses of ourselves and do something irreversible."

Laird Munro blinked at Graeme's bluntness. Jerome remained silent, watching Graeme closely, though the suspicion and anger narrowing his eyes earlier had eased slightly.

The Laird brought a hand up to the graying beard on his chin. "I hear what ye are saying, lad," he murmured. "Truth be told, that is the verra reason the Bruce called me to Lochmaben. He hopes that the Highland clans can find a way to expend less energy on our feuds so that we can face the English in a united front. We'd all hoped the war would be over with the Battle of Bannockburn, but it looks as though freedom will come slow and hard-fought."

Graeme nodded. "Aye, exactly. The King needs our best if we ever hope to defeat the English once and for all, no' all this squabbling and fighting over a dozen sheep here and there."

"Or a thwarted marriage alliance?" Jerome asked quietly, lifting a dark brow. "Some of our feuds are petty, aye, but others have run in our blood for centuries."

"Do ye want yer bairns fighting the same wars as ye, Jerome?" Graeme murmured. "Or yer grandbairns? I dinnae."

He looked at Anna again, and her pulse quickened. It felt as though they were teetering on a blade's edge.

On one side lay the familiar ways of doing things—feuds, squabbles, and long-standing tensions. If their people could not learn to get along, it wouldn't matter if the Pope himself blessed Graeme and Anna's union, and all this would be for naught.

On the other side, however, lay a future where they could live and love whom they wanted, and mayhap even find a greater strength in their unity than they ever had apart.

"Aye, our feuds run deep, but someone has to end them. Someone has to be willing to be the first," Graeme said quietly. "And I propose that we be those people."

"What are ye suggesting?" Laird Munro asked.

"That the MacKays, Munros, and Rosses all form an alliance," Graeme replied, squaring his shoulders. "My marriage to Anna will go a long way to unite our two clans. And with the Munros so close to the Rosses, yer clan would be a natural friend of the MacKays as well, Laird. Together, we'd have far greater leverage and bargaining power when it comes to dealing with the likes of the Mackenzies. Who kens, mayhap this will even ease tensions between the Rosses and the Sutherlands, what with the MacKays as a common ally."

Laird Munro considered this for a long time until Anna feared that he wouldn't even dignify such an idea with a response. At last, though, he spoke.

"Such talk is all well and good when it is just that—talk. But how do ye hope to bring this all to fruition, lad? To speak plainly, ye are neither a Laird nor the son of a Laird. What sway do ye have over such dealings?"

"I may no' be in a position of power myself. But as ye say, the King himself wishes for such alliances amongst the Highland clans," Graeme said. "My cousin, Colin MacKay, has worked closely with the King in his Bodyguard Corps, and I was set to join him in the Corps before…well, before I made a mess of things with this mission."

Graeme let out a breath that was half-mirth, half-desperation. "Even if I am no longer welcome in the Corps after…all this," he waved a hand to encompass Anna, the abbey, Jerome, and Laird

Munro, "Colin still has the King's ear. I have every faith that if it meant peace in the Highlands, the Bruce would direct Colin to speak with Laird Iye MacKay about an alliance treaty between our three clans."

Jerome leaned back in his chair then, and to Anna's shock, he actually wore a look of respect on his normally hard-set features.

Laird Munro began to nod slowly. "I believe—as does the King—that it is past time we put aside these petty differences and come together as Highlanders."

He stood slowly, and Graeme and Jerome followed suit. The Laird extended his hand toward Graeme. "For peace."

Graeme took Laird Munro's hand in a firm forearm shake.

"For peace."

Epilogue

One month later
Ross Clan Keep, Scottish Highlands

Graeme leaned back against the stone wall inside the Ross keep's great hall. He folded his arms and whistled softly through his teeth at what he was witnessing.

Laird William Ross had scribed his name on the piece of parchment spread out on the table before him, then pressed his signet ring into a glob of red wax to put his seal on the document.

Laird Ross handed the quill to Laird Donald Munro, who did the same. Munro passed the quill to Laird Iye MacKay with a serious nod, who provided the final signature and seal on the alliance treaty between the three clans.

"I never thought I'd see this day," Colin said,

coming to stand beside Graeme to watch the three Lairds exchange firm forearm shakes.

"Nor did I," Graeme murmured.

"I dinnae just mean the alliance, either," Colin said. "I mean I never thought I'd see Graeme MacKay go from blunt-tongued warrior to smooth-talking diplomat. Who kenned ye had it in ye, cousin?"

Graeme turned to find one of Colin's blond brows lifted, a taunting grin on his mouth.

This time Graeme could not control the urge to punch his cousin. Since Colin had been such a help in securing Laird MacKay's cooperation, however, he satisfied himself with pounding Colin in the shoulder rather than in that damned annoying smile of his.

Before Colin could return the blow, Jerome stepped in front of the two men. Graeme stilled, for he hadn't spoken more than a terse greeting to the man who seemed so set on disliking him.

To Graeme's shock, Jerome hesitated for a moment, then extended his hand for a shake. As Graeme clasped forearms with him, Jerome spoke quietly.

"Ye accomplished quite the feat today, MacKay," he said grudgingly. "My Laird and my people are grateful to ye."

"Thank ye," Graeme said. He couldn't help but notice that Jerome had left himself off the list of those who were grateful to him for this alliance, but knowing what a proud and stubborn warrior Jerome was, Graeme would take it as high praise.

As Jerome moved off to his Laird's side, Graeme leaned back against the stones once more. "If the Bruce is still looking for good men for his Bodyguard Corps, he'd be hard-pressed to find one better than Jerome Munro," he said, tilting his head toward Colin. "If the loyalty he's given his Laird could be harnessed for the King's missions, he'd be an unstoppable force. I certainly dinnae want to cross him again."

"I'll make sure the Bruce hears that," Colin replied. "But are ye sure Jerome would be willing to work with ye? The Bodyguard Corps is small, and the men have to be able to train together, fight together, and follow orders side by side. Jerome looks like he'd still rather knock ye around a bit for stealing his Laird's bride."

Graeme jerked up from the wall and spun to face Colin. Ignoring the teasing grin he still wore, Graeme fixed Colin with a hard stare.

"Are ye…are ye saying that I am still in the Bodyguard Corps?" Graeme breathed.

"Aye, of course, man," Colin replied easily. "Ye think the Bruce has never dealt with one of his bodyguards falling in love on a mission?" Colin snorted. "Hell, it seems to be an occupational hazard."

"But...but he tasked me with delivering Anna safely to her betrothed, and instead I kidnapped her so that I could marry her myself."

"The way Anna tells it, she went with ye willingly," Colin said, giving Graeme a sideways smirk. "Besides, ye *did* keep her safe. And though ye managed to destroy one Highland alliance, ye formed two more, so I believe the Bruce is actually quite pleased with ye."

Colin turned fully to Graeme then, his face growing serious. "Truly, Graeme, ye dinnae need to fash. The Bruce insists that ye remain in the Corps, for he wants good men like ye—men with no' just the mission in mind, but also the peace and prosperity of all of Scotland." He slapped Graeme's shoulder. "Ye did well, cousin."

Graeme felt his chest swell with pride at the praise. He'd never been more than a soldier, a warrior, until now. When his leg had been injured, he'd feared that he would be neither, that his whole life would amount to naught.

Instead, he found he'd gained so much more. He'd gained Anna as his bride, a new role in the Bruce's cause—he was even regaining strength and stability in his leg.

"Are ye staying for the feast this evening?" he asked Colin. "It promises to be one for the ages."

With Laird Ross's blessing, Graeme and Anna had agreed to hold their wedding later that evening, followed by a feast to celebrate both their union and the alliance forged between the MacKays, Rosses, and Munros. All three clans had gathered at the Ross keep, and the air nigh hummed with anticipation for the joyous occasion.

"I wouldnae miss it," Colin said.

"Good. Then I'll see ye later tonight." Graeme shoved himself off the wall and began making his way toward the doors that led from the great hall to the courtyard outside.

"Where are ye going?" Colin called behind him.

"To find my bride."

Graeme pushed through the double doors and into the bright summer sun. His gaze immediately landed on Anna, who stood at the other end of the yard with a mare on a tether. She was gently urging the mare to walk in slow circles around her.

The technique was normally used to tame wild horses, but Anna had decided to use it to instead tame her own fear of the animals. Graeme's heart filled to overflowing as he walked toward her. He hardly noticed his limp as he watched her bravely facing her fears.

When she lifted her golden head and her gaze fell on him, his breath caught in his throat. And when she gave him a smile more radiant than the sun overhead, he forgot to breathe all together.

"Are ye nervous to be around the horse?" he asked, coming to a halt before her.

She glanced at the sweet, gentle mare, then back at him, her smile widening.

"Nay."

"Then mayhap ye are anxious about tonight? Having doubts about marrying me? Or a wee bit uneasy at what will happen in our marriage bed?"

Now a bright flush of pink rose to her cheeks, sweetening her smile even more.

"Nay. No second thoughts, and no nerves for the marriage bed."

"Then why are ye smiling so fiercely, lass?" he teased, running a thumb along her heated cheek.

"Because I am happy," she replied, her blue eyes shining with emotion. "Purely, truly, and completely happy."

The End

Author's Note

As always, it's such a treat to be able to share not only an adventurous and romantic story with you, but also tell you a bit more about the history behind this tale! Although this is a work of fiction, quite a few historical tidbits shaped the story.

As far as the historical and political backdrop of wars, feuds, and alliances goes, it's true that the Munro and Ross clans have a long history of close cooperation. In 1250, almost seventy years before this story takes place, William, the son of the Earl of Ross at the time, was kidnapped in an uprising against the Earl's rule. The Munros helped rescue the Earl of Ross's son, thus sealing a tight and long-standing union between the two clans.

And although smaller feuds always existed between many Highland clans, the Rosses, Munros, and MacKays all joined Robert the Bruce against

AUTHOR'S NOTE

the English, though they all took slightly different routes in their support of the Bruce's cause.

The Munros sided with the Bruce well before the Battle of Bannockburn, a decisive and pivotal victory in the Scottish cause for independence. Robert Munro, the Munro clan's chief in the early 1300s, fought with his son George alongside the Bruce at Bannockburn in 1314. Robert survived, but George gave his life to the cause.

And while the MacKays supported the Bruce's efforts almost from the beginning, the Rosses took a slightly more winding path. The Rosses fought against the English at the Battle of Dunbar in 1296, but in the battle, the chief of the clan, Uilleam II, was captured. For a short time after that, Uilleam supported the English, but then changed allegiances back to the Scots, leading the Rosses to fight on the side of the Bruce in the Battle of Bannockburn as well. Uilliam's son, Hugh (or Aodh), was a favorite of the Bruce's, and Hugh/Aodh eventually married the Bruce's sister, Matilda. So even with some clan feuding, all three clans were tightly interwoven with each other and Robert the Bruce's fight for freedom.

A quick note on the three Lairds' names. Uilliam II of Ross became Laird William Ross in this story. I chose the name Donald for Laird Munro because Donald Munro was said to be the founder of the Munro clan back in the twelfth

AUTHOR'S NOTE

century. And Iye MacKay was the name of the founder of the MacKay clan in the early thirteenth century—plus it was the name of five subsequent chiefs of the clan as well!

Regarding the reading of the banns, secret engagements, and how to get out of an arranged marriage, there are quite a few fun historical tidbits to share. The reading of the banns become customary starting in the twelfth and thirteenth centuries. For three consecutive Sundays after an engagement was made public, an announcement would be made during church about the impending wedding, and any objections were meant to be brought forward then. (It was kind of like a preemptory "speak now or forever hold your peace" moment, but it lasted for three weeks before the wedding rather than just one moment during the ceremony.)

Though some couples didn't follow the church's rules (in some times and places, simply declaring that you were now married in front of a witness was enough, and declaring that you were married and then having sex made it *extra* official!), the church sought to funnel all marriages through an approved series of rules and steps. Partly this was to avoid he-said-she-said disputes about couples claiming to be either married or not married, depending on what one person in the couple wanted to do (like marry someone else). It was also a chance to avoid consan-

AUTHOR'S NOTE

guinity (the couple being too closely related by blood), or to air out any standing engagements that would void the marriage.

While researching another book a while back, I came across the story of Joan of Kent and knew I had to work this particularly interesting historical oddity into one of my stories. Joan of Kent eventually married Edward the Black Prince and became the mother of the future King Richard II. But before that, she was married in her teens with the reading of the banns beforehand, a full church service—the works. Yet after eight years of marriage, the union was found to be unlawful because before her official wedding, she had secretly married a knight without her family's knowledge or approval when she was just twelve. That earlier marriage voided the later one, despite the fact that she had been living as a married woman with her "second" husband for eight years.

I tweaked that slightly here to introduce the idea that in addition to an earlier marriage, a pre-standing engagement was grounds to void any later engagements or marriage. That's just what the reading of the banns was for—to give the public three weeks to voice any reason why a couple could not be legally wed.

A note about Sweetheart Abbey—it is a real place, located south of Dumfries and not far from Lochmaben. Its official name is Abbey of Dolce

Cor (sweet heart in Latin), though it is better known as Sweetheart Abbey.

It was built out of dark red sandstones in 1275 at the request of Dervorguilla of Galloway in memory of her late husband, Baron John de Balliol. When John died, Dervorguilla asked that his heart be embalmed and placed in a casket of ivory and silver, which she kept with her for the rest of her life. After she died, John's heart was buried alongside her in Sweetheart Abbey, which she named knowing that she would take her final rest with her late husband there. John and Dervorguilla's son, John Balliol, would eventually become the King of Scotland, though his reign was short-lived and troubled, for his rival was none other than Robert the Bruce.

Astute readers will remember that Dervorguilla made an appearance in the Author's Note after *Heart's Thief* (Highland Bodyguards, Book 2) for building Dervorguilla's Bridge. She was a powerful figure in thirteenth-century Scotland, especially around Dumfries where she lived.

Sweetheart Abbey was damaged during the Scottish wars for independence, and later when it was struck by lightning, but its ruins still stand and you can visit the aptly named abbey today.

And one last note just for fun. Graeme says he would have been turned into a pin-pillow by English archers if he hadn't been saved after being

AUTHOR'S NOTE

shot with an arrow. A pin-pillow was one of the medieval names for (can you guess?) a pincushion. Pincushions have been around in Europe since at least the 1300s—who knew?

    Thank you for journeying back to medieval Scotland with me!

Make sure to sign up for my newsletter to hear about all my sales, giveaways, and new releases. Plus, get exclusive content like stories, excerpts, cover reveals, and more. Sign up at www.EmmaPrinceBooks.com

Thank You!

Thank you for taking the time to read *A Highland Betrothal* (Highland Bodyguards, Book 4.5)!

And thank you in advance for sharing your enjoyment of this book (or my other books) with fellow readers by leaving a review on Amazon. Long or short, detailed or to the point, I read all reviews and greatly appreciate you for writing one!

I love connecting with readers! Sign up for my newsletter and be the first to hear about my latest book news, flash sales, giveaways, and more—signing up is free and easy at www.EmmaPrinceBooks.com.

You also can join me on Twitter at: @EmmaPrinceBooks.

Or keep up on Facebook at: https://www.facebook.com/EmmaPrinceBooks.

TEASERS FOR EMMA PRINCE'S BOOKS

Highland Bodyguards Series:

The Lady's Protector, the thrilling start to the Highland Bodyguards series, is available now on Amazon.

The Battle of Bannockburn may be over, but the war is far from won.

Her Protector…

Ansel Sutherland is charged with a mission from King Robert the Bruce to protect the illegitimate son of a powerful English Earl. Though Ansel bristles at aiding an Englishman, the nature of the war for Scottish independence is changing, and he is honor-bound to serve as a bodyguard. He arrives in England to fulfill his assignment, only to meet the beautiful but secretive Lady Isolda, who refuses to tell him where his ward is. When a mysterious attacker threatens Isolda's life, Ansel realizes he is the only thing standing between her and deadly peril.

His Lady...

Lady Isolda harbors dark secrets—secrets she refuses to reveal to the rugged Highland rogue who arrives at her castle demanding answers. But Ansel's dark eyes cut through all her defenses, threatening to undo her resolve. To protect her past, she cannot submit to the white-hot desire that burns between them. As the threat to her life spirals out of control, she has no choice but to trust Ansel to whisk her to safety deep in the heart of the Highlands...

Have your heart stolen by Colin and Sabine's story in **_Heart's Thief_ (Highland Bodyguards, Book 2)**. Available now on Amazon.

A dangerous mission…

Although Colin MacKay is thought a charmer, he hides an old wound behind his quick smile and dancing blue eyes. To ease the pain of a past betrayal, he has devoted his life to the cause for Scottish freedom. When King Robert the Bruce fears his strategic communications have been compromised, he sends Colin on a crucial mission: ferret out the spy and deliver an urgent missive to the King's brother. When Colin discovers that the deceptively enchanting Sabine has been intercepting the King's correspondence, he holds her captive until he can deliver his missive and hand her over to the King's judgement. But detaining the sable-haired beauty proves far more dangerous when lust flares hot between them.

A deadly game of seduction...

Sabine has known only the life of a thief. Scooped from the streets as an orphan child, she thinks of the man who saved her as a father, though his dark moods and cruel manipulations keep her frightened of being abandoned again. Under his tutelage, she learns that with a suggestive smile or a heart-wrenching tale, she can lower men's guards just long enough to steal their secrets. But when she is sent to seduce a handsome, golden-maned Highlander bearing a message from the Bruce, soon she cannot tell who is playing whom, or if it is a game at all. Colin's searing touch crumbles the walls around her heart, forcing Sabine to realize that her loyalty to her boss may come with a price—her life. When unseen forces threaten to tear their world apart, Sabine and Colin must choose between duty, loyalty, and love to save themselves—and each other.

Meet Graeme MacKay for the first time and learn more about the siege on Berwick Castle in Kirk's story, ***Claimed by the Bounty Hunter*** (**Highland Bodyguards, Book 4**). Available now on Amazon.

To protect his cover, he must claim her as his captive. To save her own life, she must claim his heart...

A gruesome siege destroys Kirk MacLeod's faith in the Scottish fight for independence. Robert the Bruce promises to release Kirk from his service if he completes one final assignment: infiltrate the deadly bounty hunter league that has thwarted the Scots' cause for years. Kirk plays the part of a cold-blooded mercenary almost too well. But when the league orders him to kidnap a beautiful English-woman, he must choose between following his mission and following his heart.

Lillian Fitzhugh's late husband leaves her with a powerful secret—one that has men willing to capture and kill for it. When she's taken by Kirk, a ruthless Highland bounty hunter set to deliver her to the men who murdered her husband, she fears all is lost. But she senses that beneath her captor's hardened exterior lies the heart of an honorable man. To gain her freedom, she must unravel the truth of Kirk's identity. In doing so, she ensnares them both in a dangerous web of desire and secrets that may cost them both their lives.

The Sinclair Brothers Trilogy:

Go back to where it all began—with Robert and Alwin's story in **Highlander's Ransom**, Book One of the Sinclair Brothers Trilogy. Available now on Amazon.

He was out for revenge...

Laird Robert Sinclair would stop at nothing to exact revenge on Lord Raef Warren, the English scoundrel who had brought war to his doorstep and razed his lands and people. Leaving his clan in the Highlands to conduct covert attacks in the Borderlands, Robert lives to be a thorn in Warren's side. So when he finds a beautiful English lass on her way to marry Warren, he whisks her away to the Highlands with a plan to ransom her back to her dastardly fiancé.

She would not be controlled...

Lady Alwin Hewett had no idea when she left her father's manor to marry a man she'd never met that she would instead be kidnapped by a Highland rogue out for vengeance. But she refuses to be a pawn in any man's game. So when she learns that Robert has had them secretly wed, she will stop at nothing to regain her freedom. But her heart may have other plans...

About the Author

Emma Prince is the Bestselling and Amazon All-Star Author of steamy historical romances jam-packed with adventure, conflict, and of course, love!

Emma grew up in drizzly Seattle, but traded her rain boots for sunglasses when she and her husband moved to the eastern slopes of the Sierra Nevada. Emma spent several years in academia, both as a graduate student and an instructor of college-level

English and Humanities courses. She always savored her "fun books"—normally historical romances—on breaks or vacations. But as she began looking for the next chapter in her life, she wondered if perhaps her passion could turn into a career. Ever since then, she's been reading and writing books that celebrate happily ever afters!

Visit Emma's website, www.EmmaPrinceBooks.com, for updates on new books, future projects, her newsletter sign-up, book extras, and more!

You can follow Emma on Twitter at: @EmmaPrinceBooks.

Or join her on Facebook at: www.facebook.com/EmmaPrinceBooks.

Made in the USA
Monee, IL
25 June 2021